P9-DCZ-718

Evil Returns

Caroline B. Cooney
AR B.L.: 4.6
Points: 5.0   UG

THE VAMPIRE'S PROMISE #2

EVIL RETURNS

CAROLINE B. COONEY

SCHOLASTIC INC.

New York Toronto London Auckland Sydney
Mexico City New Delhi Hong Kong Buenos Aires

B

T 31544

No part of this publication may be reproduced in whole or in part, or stored in a retrieval system, or transmitted in any form or by any means, electronic, mechanical, photocopying, recording, or otherwise, without written permission of the publisher. For information regarding permission, write to Scholastic Inc., Attention: Permissions Department, 557 Broadway, New York, NY 10012.

ISBN 0-439-55396-2

Copyright © 1992 by Caroline B. Cooney.

All rights reserved.
Published by Scholastic Inc., 557 Broadway,
New York, NY 10012.
SCHOLASTIC and associated logos are trademarks
and/or registered trademarks of Scholastic Inc.

12 11 10 9 8 7 6 5 4 3 2   4 5 6 7 8/0

Printed in the U.S.A.
First Scholastic printing, February 1992

Originally titled *Return of the Vampire*

Chapter 1

"I don't think I want to sleep in the tower after all," Devnee said to her parents.

"Devnee," said her father. He was really quite annoyed. "Half the reason we bought the house was because you wanted a bedroom in a tower."

They had rejected raised ranches, Cape Cods, and bungalows and bought a dark Victorian mansion in desperate need of repair. Mr. Fountain wanted the workshop in the high dry cellar. Mrs. Fountain wanted the glassed-in room to raise flowers. Luke wanted the yard so he could play basketball, baseball, and football.

But Devnee had wanted the tower. How romantic a tower had sounded! Her own castle, her own corner of the sky. She would fling open the windows and a blue sky and a gentle sun would welcome her to a new town. She would curl up on her sleigh bed to read books, and she would brush her hair in front of a mirror with a white wicker frame, and somehow this time, in this town, this year, she would be beautiful and she would be popular and happy.

The tower jutted out of the attic, but was not part of it. It had a separate stair up from the second floor. The tower was round, and its plaster walls were cracked, its windows tightly shuttered.

Shuttered on the inside.

Devnee had never come across shutters on the inside of a house. Their new home had shutters all over the outside — louvered, broken shutters that banged in the wind and creaked in the night. But the tower had another set on the inside, strapped down with black metal, as if the tower had once held prisoners. "We'll just quick flip open these shutters," her father had said yesterday afternoon, nudging at the hasps and bolts, "and then the sunlight will stream into your new bedroom, Dev!"

But the armor of the shutters would not come free, and the moving men had been downstairs yelling where did Mr. Fountain want the leather recliner, and he had said he would get to the shutters later.

They had moved her bed into the tower. It was a romantic bed, with its sleigh back and lacy white ruffle, high mattress, and sheets with dark mysterious flowers. They had moved her chest of drawers into the tower. The chest was narrow and had seven drawers; Devnee was not tall enough to see into the top one. She also had a chair, a computer, and a sound system, but they were still sitting in the downstairs hall. There had not been enough time to move them into the tower.

The moving men left.

Her parents and her brother, Luke, were starving and insisted on going into town for something to eat.

Devnee made her first serious mistake. She told them to go without her, and bring her back a hamburger and french fries. She would stay alone in the house, and get to know her new room, and the new smell, and the new feel of life in a different state.

She did not know, last night, how different a state could be.

Luke and her mother and her father chattered steadily as they went to the car. The doors of the car slammed, and the engine of the car growled, and Devnee Fountain was alone in a house with a tower.

Devnee played the game she always played when she was alone. The beautiful game. Where the lovely funny terrific girl on the inside finally had a match on the outside; where Devnee's hair gleamed, and her smile sparkled, and her personality captivated.

She had left the kitchen. Kitchens were no place to play the beautiful game. Kitchens, like Devnee, were useful and stodgy.

She would go to the tower to be beautiful.

No one knew about the game. Devnee was so

dull and plain that people would have laughed at the mere suggestion of beauty, and then smothered the laughter in pity.

She left the kitchen and walked into the large high-ceilinged center hallway, where the wallpaper was stained from the squares of long-gone portraits. She stood on the bottom step of the wide stairs that led to the second floor.

Perhaps this time she would play bride. Or prom queen.

She pretended to fling a mass of shining hair and to widen eyes that stopped boys in their tracks.

Reality taunted Devnee Fountain. *Right,* it said. *You? Beautiful?*

I don't want beauty to be a game! she thought. I want it to be real. I want to be beautiful for real.

A sort of reverse gravity began to pull at Devnee Fountain. The backs of her eyes and the roots of her hair leaned toward the tower. Her fingers crawled up the banister and dragged her arms after them. The stairs disappeared behind her. Her hand stuck to the round glass knob of the door that opened to the tower stair. Her head went up ahead of her, but her feet argued and hung back and tried to turn around. Her eyes leaped forward.

The stairwell breathed. It filled its lungs like a runner after a race. Devnee's lungs did not fill at all. She caved in. She cried out.

And she climbed on, equal parts wind and weight.

It was darker in the tower than anyplace Devnee had ever been. The dark had textures, some velvet, some satin. The dark shifted positions.

The dark continued to breathe. The breath of the tower lifted her clothing like the flaps of a tent, and snuffled in her ears like falling snow.

It's the wind coming through the double shutters, Devnee told herself.

But how could wind come through? There were glass windows between the outside and inside shutters.

Or were there?

The windows weren't just holes in the wall, were they?

What if there was no glass? What if things crawled through those open louvers, crept into the room, blew in with the cold that fingered her hair? What creatures of the night could slither through those slats?

She had not realized how wonderful glass was, how it protected you and kept you inside.

There must be glass, Devnee thought. Something has to stand between me and — and what? What do I think is out there, except the night air?

She knew that something was out there.

She could hear it, crawling on the roof, filtering through the louvers.

Devnee put her hands out to feel the shutters.

In front of her face appeared some other hand. A hand with long fingernails of silver, wrinkled like crushed foil. Fingernails poked toward her, eager and grasping. The hand shifted the dark as if stirring ingredients, and it crossed the room toward Devnee like a growing stalk.

Her own hands rose like vapor. Devnee knew she was going to hold hands with the hand.

Devnee jerked her hands back, and tucked them under her arms for safekeeping, and staggered to the tower door. Stumbling and sick, she half fell, half flew down the tower stairs, down the second-floor stairs, throwing herself into the kitchen just as her brother came in with her bag of food.

"Hungry, huh?" said Luke, tossing it to her.

As she caught the paper bag with its red-and-gold logo it seemed to her that a second pair of hands also closed around the food: hands with fingernails so yellow and tarnished they were like old teeth in need of brushing.

Who is in this house with me? thought Devnee Fountain. Who lives between those shutters?

"If you're not going to eat that, I will," said Luke.

"She's nervous about her first day in a new school tomorrow," said their mother affectionately and soothingly. "Everybody to bed now. A good night's sleep is what we all need, and we'll worry about the rest of the furniture later on."

Devnee managed to smile. Her parents did not approve of complaining. They called it "whining" and felt that high school girls like Devnee should not whine.

So Devnee tried not to. "It's kind of creepy up there," she said, striving to sound careless and relaxed. "I don't think I want to sleep in the tower after all."

Her mother frowned. "It'll be a darling, darling little room once we have it fixed up. I see it in peach and ivory. It cries out for soft pastel colors."

It cries out for me, thought Devnee.

"The thing is, Dev, we have to do the kitchen first. That's our priority. Once we have sinks and cabinets and a new shiny vinyl floor, we can think about things like painting the bedrooms." Her mother smiled, a secret smile, her daydreaming smile. Devnee's mother daydreamed of things like remodeling. She could hardly wait to go from store to store, studying samples of vinyl floor coverings. Her mother would actually say out loud, "Doesn't it shine?" and "Do you really like this new finish?"

Devnee looked at her family: sturdy father, overgrown weed of a brother, domestic mother. Her father loved television; her brother loved sports; her mother loved cooking.

This was her life. This was the family she had drawn.

How she wished for something more special! People who did not fit into such suburban stereotypes. People with personality and pizzazz. But this was the right family for her; she was just as dull and predictable. Plain brown hair, plain pale face, plain ordinary smile, plain acceptable clothing.

Devnee crumpled the hamburger bag and dropped it in the garbage. She felt crumpled herself, exhausted from the silly beautiful game, the dumb tricks of her imagination, the nonsense of a tower that breathed.

And so Devnee went up to the tower again.

Night went on.

Sleep did not come.

Something damp and gelatinous brushed over her face.

Devnee cried out, and a hand clamped down over her mouth. Not her own hand — some other hand: cold and horny and soft like rotting fruit; as if it would burst and evil would spill out.

Devnee ripped the hand away from her mouth, whirled in the bed, and reached for the light switch on the wall. The blessed shape of the switch; the hard ivory-colored plastic. She flicked it up, and the room turned yellow and bright.

Her heart was beating as fast as a rabbit's.

Nothing was there. No thickness in the shadows. No movement by the shutters. Nothing damp and nothing rotting soft.

The only hands were her own, clutching the sheet hem as if she were a sailor for Columbus, falling off the edge of the world.

Calm down, Devnee told herself. You're just worried about the first day of school tomorrow. That's all. You gave yourself the heebie-jeebies.

For a long time she looked around the room, to see if anything came out of the cracks.

Gradually she relaxed against the pillows.

The room would be fine once the shutters were opened, pretty lacy curtains were hung, a rug put down. Once the plaster was repaired and the walls painted. Yes. She would choose cheery daytime colors and the rug would be thick and cozy-soft under her toes.

Devnee yawned, trying to entice sleep. Then she stretched, trying to get ready to lie back down. At last she folded her hands on her chest, to calm herself. I must look like a corpse laid out, thought Devnee.

She glanced down to see how she looked, and she saw something that could not be.

Her shadow had not folded its hands.

Her shadow was not attached to her.

Her shadow was on the far side of the room, exploring by itself, its black elongated fingers, like the tines of an immense fork, raking silently over door cracks and shutter louvers.

She tried to breathe, but the room itself was breathing so much it sucked up all the air. There was none left for her. She tried to think, but the ancient thoughts of all the people who had ever used the tower were swirling in the air, and she had no thoughts of her own.

Mommy, she whimpered soundlessly. *Daddy, Luke.*

Something came toward her, but it was not Mommy or Daddy or Luke.

"Come here," Devnee whispered to her shadow.

But it did not come.

If I turn off the light, thought Devnee, that would end my shadow.

But the darkness of the tower was so full of shape and texture and edge. Perhaps the shadow would stay alive even in the dark. Cruising through the room. Touching things. Touching perhaps Devnee's own cheek in the dark.

I'll close my eyes, thought Devnee, and calm myself down. This is not happening, and when I open my eyes, it will be an ordinary room with an ordinary shadow attached to my ordinary body.

But the experiment did not work, and she did not stay calm and serene.

The night was long.

A sort of dark path was lit across the room, leading to the shutters. She did not get out of the bed to follow the path. Her feet were bare, and the wood floor would be cold as pond ice in January. And the path — who knew where it led?

When Devnee awoke in the morning, the bedroom light was off.

At breakfast she said, "Did you come up and turn my light off, Mom?"

"No, darling."

"Did you, Daddy?"

"Nope."

She didn't ask Luke. Luke slept like a brick, which reflected his brainpower and personality. Even if every light in the house were on at two in the morning, Luke would never think of turning them off. Luke did not do a lot of thinking. Devnee was not sure her brother would think of mentioning fire if the house went up in flames. Luke was a big lug who played ball, and that was the limit of his mastery of the world.

In the kitchen, among the debris of remodeling and the mess of their first breakfast, she felt safe and warm. What could go wrong in a room that smelled of pancakes and maple syrup? Last night was not worth thinking about. There was too much of today to worry over.

Devnee had had difficulty deciding what to wear. Would this be a school in which girls dressed sloppily, with torn sneakers, too-big sweatshirts, old jeans? Or would they look chic? Or preppy? Or some style she had never encountered before?

Schools should send a video before you enrolled, so you could see how the kids dressed, and not get it wrong.

But then, what did it matter if Devnee Fountain got her clothes wrong?

She might be going to a new school, but she had her same old looks.

I wish . . . thought Devnee, aching to be a different person. The kind of girl who made people light up and turn to face her and call out her nickname when she walked in. A beautiful girl.

If you were beautiful, everything came with it: friends, laughter, company.

This was her chance! Her chance as the new girl to start a new life.

Oh, let it be a *better* life!

It was early; they did not have to leave for school yet.

Devnee walked outside. She did not know why. She was not an outdoor person. Certainly not in winter. Something drew her.

How cold it was in the yard. Frost during the night had whitened the grass, and water in a tilted old birdbath was frozen. The high hedge of hemlocks that encircled the mansion was more black than green, and the winter morning sky was not sunny, just less dark.

When you wish upon a star . . . Devnee sang to herself.

No wind, and no clouds. Just a faceless gray morning and a queer damp chill. She felt she should not stay outdoors too long or moss might grow on her face.

Devnee looked up at her tower and the moment her gaze landed on the circling shutters, one of them banged.

But there was no wind.

The shutter banged a second time, and the broken louvers on the shutter seemed to curve upward in a secret smile.

Devnee kicked her shoe in the dirt. She had decided on sneakers that looked like leather: black ones, quite new, but not new enough to look desperate. They would blend with any fashion.

But I don't want to blend in! thought Devnee, as filled with pain as a heart attack patient. I want to be beautiful!

I wish . . . she thought forlornly.

Devnee had not put on a coat. The chill wrapped around her, as if it had folds and fabric, like a winter coat. The chill warmed her. It was as if she had become some strange new animal and the blood in her veins would decide what was warm.

Cold was warm.

If cold can be warm, thought Devnee, perhaps plain can be beautiful. How I want to be beautiful!

Even her knuckles and fingers begged for beauty, turning white, clasping each other, beseeching the powers that be to turn Devnee Fountain into a beautiful girl.

The wish was not mild and passing.

It was sharp, intense. Every girl, every day, wishes for changes in her body, or her heart, or her life. But few wished so desperately as Devnee Fountain.

Devnee went back inside, into the warmth.

Her words lay on the air.

I wish . . .

The wish left, as her shadow had, and went on without her.

In the darkness of the hemlocks around the

mansion, against the dark shingles of the house, more darkness gathered. Thicker darkness. A darkness both velvety and satiny.

The dark path caught the wish and kept it.

Something bright glittered in the branches of the hemlocks, like a row of tiny silver bells.

Or fingernails, wrinkled like old foil.

The dark path curled around the base of a tree, and waited for the rest of the wish.

Chapter 2

Back at the breakfast table, nobody had moved.

Her mother was still pouring orange juice into the same glass.

The juice seemed to slide out of the cardboard box and into the glass forever and ever, as if her mother was just a hand holding a pitcher.

Her father was still holding a fork above his pancakes, and her brother was still lifting his napkin.

Devnee shivered.

Had she gone outside at all? What had happened to the time she had spent out there? Was it her time only, and had it not existed for the three inside the house? What was happening in this house, that time flickered differently wherever you stood, and fingernails crept out of cracks, and shadows peeled away from your body?

"I want to sleep downstairs in the guest room," Devnee said, and the family stirred slightly, as if waking up.

"Dev," said her mother, "no. We have all kinds of guests coming. You know that. Nobody in our family has ever lived in this part of the country before, and they're *dying* to visit. The little guest room is the boring room, nobody wants it full-time, and we agreed that's where we'll stuff the guests."

Luke said, "Wouldn't it be weird if the guests really did die when they came to visit? And we really did stuff them?"

Devnee could not breathe.

"Luke, try to be human," said their mother.

I wonder which of us is human, thought Devnee. I wonder if I'm human. My shadow isn't human. But then, shadows aren't human, she realized.

So why did my shadow make choices of its own? Exploring and wandering? It shouldn't be doing anything I don't do.

Devnee said, "I don't want to start school here yet."

"State laws," said her mother cheerfully. "You have to start school today. I'll drive you, since it's your first day, and you run down and check in the office and see what the nearest bus route is for tomorrow."

Her mother made "checking in the office" sound as easy as ordering a hamburger, but it wouldn't be. It would be strange halls and a thousand strange faces. Doors that were not marked clearly and people who spoke too loudly or not at all, while Devnee shuffled her feet like a broken-down ballerina.

She almost wished that she and Luke were in the same school. Then she would have company on the horrible first day in a new school.

On the other hand, who would want Luke's company for anything? It was good that he was still in ninth grade and in this town that meant junior high, while she was safely in tenth grade, and far superior to her dumb brother.

They dropped off Luke first, because the junior high was closer, and Luke bounded in as if he had always gone there, and already had friends and already knew the way to the gym and where the cafeteria line began.

What if I don't have friends here ever? thought Devnee.

What if it's a horrible hateful mean place and I'm dressed wrong? And they laugh at me?

When they arrived at the high school, Devnee's mother came in with her after all. Devnee, who adored her mother, was ashamed: Mrs. Fountain was quite heavy and needed a new, larger winter coat. Instead of taking the time to curl her hair, her mother had just tugged it back into a loose, messy ponytail.

As if taking Devnee to her first day in a new school in a new town didn't matter.

Devnee swallowed the thought and tried to stay loyal.

She glanced behind her to see if her shadow had come along and it had. It seemed curiously large for Devnee, and too dark for the thin, shivering sun of January. It seemed like somebody else's shadow.

Immediately she knew that it *was* somebody else's. It was the shadow of the fingernails, with talons like a hawk's. She forced herself to stare straight ahead. She was not going to collapse because the tower had switched shadows on her during the night. She had a first day of school to get through.

In the office, the secretary did not even look up at them. "New student?" she said in a tight, snappish voice. "What grade, please? What courses were you taking at your previous school, please? Do you have your health papers showing you are properly inoculated?" Now she looked up, scanning Devnee for disease-carrying properties. Devnee tried to look clean and healthy.

Her mother said, "Wonderful!" though what she could be referring to, Devnee could not imagine. "I'll see you after school," trilled her mother. "I'll pick you up in the front drive, darling. Have such fun!"

The secretary was wearing little half glasses, which she tilted lower on her nose to study Mrs. Fountain's exit, perfectly aware that "having such fun" was unlikely.

The secretary finished up doing important things, while Devnee leaned on the counter, wanting to die, and then at last the secretary gave her directions to the guidance office, where they would set up her schedule and take her to her first class.

The directions were so complex Devnee felt they probably led to China, not down the hall. She was close to tears, and the chilly damp of last night had come back and was penetrating her brain, making it hard to think or move.

"Oh, all right," said the secretary, "I'll take you there."

But the guidance person, a man named Fuzz (which surely could not have been the case; it was Devnee's hearing that had gotten fuzzy because she was so nervous) was quite sweet. "We have a buddy system for newcomers," said Fuzz affectionately. "We don't want anybody lost in the cracks at our school!"

The expression took on a sick reality. It seemed to Devnee that the linoleum squares parted, and huge cracks opened up, black ones filled with other people's shadows, sticky and gooey, waiting for her to step wrong.

Fuzz had a long stride, and Devnee a short one, so she was forced to gallop alongside him. Out of breath and terrified, she arrived at her first class several paces behind, as if her leash had broken. "Devnee, Devnee," he called, like a dog owner.

Devnee tried to look at the class but it was impossible. There were too many students, all staring at her, with that settled, certain-sure look of kids who had been here forever and didn't approve of newcomers.

She felt unbearably plain and dull. She could feel their eyes raking over her, losing interest immediately, because she was not beautiful, and not worth attention.

She was perilously close to tears.

"Devnee has just moved here!" said Fuzz. His voice wafted in and out of her consciousness. "Now we want Devnee to feel at home here, don't we, people?"

Nobody responded.

Fuzz read Devnee's schedule out loud, demanding that anybody with matching classes should respond and volunteer to be Devnee's buddy.

Amazingly, there were three volunteers.

Seats were shuffled so that Devnee was sitting among her "buddies."

Two girls and a boy.

She immediately forgot their names and hated herself for being a stupid worthless pitiful excuse for a human being. Probably why my shadow left, thought Devnee. Needed a better body to attach itself to.

Class ended in another quarter hour, and Devnee was not even sufficiently tuned in to figure out what subject it had been. "I'm your first buddy," said one of the girls, touching Devnee's arm and smiling at her. "I'll take you on to biology lab, and then Trey will pick you up for English and lunch."

The girl — if you could use such a boring word for this breathtaking creature — was achingly lovely.

All willowy and delicate adjectives applied to her: She was fragile, in a dark silken blouse with a long chiffon skirt swirling below. Her soft black hair was perfectly cut to fall swoopingly over her forehead and skid around her pretty ears; the back was very short, with a single wave. She seemed far older than Devnee would ever be, a sophisticated fragile creature. And yet she seemed far younger, caught in some wonderful warp of innocence and perfection, before the world touched her, before pain and loss.

"My name is Aryssa," said the girl softly, and her voice, too, was beautiful, as if she possessed a velvet throat.

Now there really were tears in Devnee's eyes. Tears of shame that she herself was so dull compared to this princess, and tears of joy that this princess had volunteered to be her buddy.

What a wonderful word — buddy.

There was hope in the world after all.

And then the boy — Trey — smiled at Devnee, too, waving good-bye, promising to be at the biology lab door, and then he would stand in the cafeteria line with her. He was not at all handsome, not the way Aryssa was beautiful. But he was what Luke would have yearned to be: utterly male and muscular and tall and slightly ferocious. His smile was vaguely threatening, as if she'd better stand in the cafeteria line the way he told her to stand or else.

The physical perfection of her two buddies overwhelmed her.

The girl buddy — whose name Devnee had already forgotten — talked about many things, giving Devnee tips for locker use, gym showers, and so forth. Devnee's brain had not gone into gear and she could not get a grip. She smiled brightly and desperately. She knew she looked like a fool.

"Hey, Aryssa," said several people, waving and beaming.

Aryssa, Devnee repeated to herself. Aryssa, Aryssa. I have to remember that. I will remember that. I have a three-syllable brain.

She and Aryssa went into biology lab together. Aryssa introduced Devnee all around. The teacher welcomed her and gave her a textbook and a lab notebook, and Devnee found herself on a stool in front of a dead frog.

While the teacher discussed dissection methods, Devnee took the opportunity to study Aryssa.

Aryssa was very preoccupied with her beauty. How could she not be? There was so much of it.

Aryssa would run the tip of her tongue over her upper lip, as if savoring her own taste and shape. She would flip her gleaming hair back with her left hand, tuck it behind her ear, and sort of kiss the air when the black locks immediately fell back where they had been. Her face was constantly in motion, it never fell into repose.

In her right hand, Aryssa held a designer pencil: tiny gold stars on silver, which she flipped between her fingers like a miniature baton.

Her hands, too, were lovely: slender and aristocratic and with perfect nails and polish that probably never chipped.

"You'll do the frog, won't you?" whispered Aryssa. Now she smiled, and the row of white teeth and the turn of red lips overwhelmed Devnee.

"Of course," said Devnee, and she did the entire lab, even doing all the notes and answers, because Aryssa clearly used her pencil only for effect, not for writing things down.

"You're a sweetie," whispered Aryssa. She actually patted Devnee's knee, and again Devnee felt like a dog on a leash. It was just that Fuzz had turned her over to a new mistress, and from now on Aryssa would lead her.

Devnee blinked back the tears. She was jealous now, too, and it was a horrible feeling, rather like the formaldehyde in which the frog was pickled; it was liquid bathing her heart, this jealousy.

Oh, to be beautiful like Aryssa!

What a pair we must make, thought Devnee sadly. Beauty and the beast.

The teacher talked for several minutes about the next step, and Devnee had time to look around. She felt safe with the high lab table in front of her, and her feet tucked around the stool, and the sharp steel scalpel in her hand. She studied the rest of the girls in the lab.

Well, she was not a beast. No, Devnee was average in this particular class; half the girls were plainer than she. Stubbier, thicker, duller.

But she remained average.

Mediocre.

Whoever set that as a goal?

Devnee forgot the dead frog and stared at Aryssa, thinking, *If only I could look just like that* . . .

I wish . . .

She tried not to complete the wish. She tried to be satisfied with her lot in life.

She failed.

I wish I were beautiful!

How satisfying it sounded. What a deep intense relief to have said the whole wish, let all her pain out, let the powers that be know what she yearned for, ached for.

I wish I were beautiful!

She felt much better for having wished; it was as cathartic as a good cry in the night. She brightened and went on with her work.

The wish — complete — entire — slid out of the schoolroom to the dark path waiting outside, where it was swallowed up, and taken home, and caressed.

Chapter 3

Aryssa sighed in relief when biology lab ended. Even her sigh was lovely, as if her soft pink lungs expired only the finest air. "This is my second time taking biology," confided Aryssa. "I just can't seem to pass a science class. I don't like thinking about any of that science stuff anyway. It makes me nervous. I don't think it's fair to have to know what's under the skin."

Devnee could identify with that.

Aryssa stroked her own hand, admiring her skin, taking pleasure in a beauty so pure it was like ice: something to skate on, something only Aryssa would ever be. The world could witness, but not have, such beauty.

But Devnee was thrilled to be addressed in that confiding voice. Even though it would cast Devnee in that always-to-be-pitied role of dull escort next to shining star, she wanted to be friends with Aryssa. "What *do* you like thinking about?" she said, to keep the conversation going.

Aryssa considered this tough question while they gathered their books and walked to the door. Devnee's second buddy was already there. Trey. Devnee gulped slightly. Two such perfect humans, and for a day, for a passing period, for lunch, they were there for her.

I wish it would last, thought Devnee.

She had a weird sense that her wishes were actually being addressed to Somebody; that Somebody was listening; that Something was happening.

Aryssa literally took Devnee's hand and stuck it in Trey's.

Trey laughed. His laughter was neither kind nor unkind, but removed, not worried about the things Devnee worried about: looks and popularity and strength and friends. "I don't think Devnee needs that much help to find the next class, Aryssa." He let go of Devnee's hand. Her hand stayed warm and tingly where he had momentarily pressed it.

Aryssa said seriously, "I didn't want anybody to get confused. This buddy system, you know — people forget who goes with who."

"You and your room temperature IQ," said Trey. "Normal people don't forget."

Aryssa's was the contented laugh of a beautiful girl who doesn't care in the least about her lack of brains — because it doesn't matter in the least.

It's not fair, thought Devnee. Aryssa doesn't need to do anything but stand there and people adore her, while I have to struggle with everything from mascara to homework just to get noticed. She wished that Trey had not let go of her hand. She wished that she could be as beautiful as Aryssa and have people speak to her so indulgently, so affectionately.

"See you tomorrow, Devnee," Aryssa said. She ran her hand lightly over Devnee's shoulders, not a hug, but sweet, passing affection.

The knife of jealousy vanished, replaced by yearning for friendship. But there would be no friendships. She knew too well the realities of high school. Her buddies would not last. They would be shepherds for a day or two and then forget her.

I am a forgettable girl, thought Devnee, and this time the jealousy sliced her heart into thin ragged strips of pain.

Aryssa looked carefully around the hallway and drifted to the right, skirt wafting, hair shining. Trey caught her arm and turned her around. Aryssa, nodding gratefully, set off in the new direction.

"She's great to look at," Trey said, eyes following Aryssa in admiration, "but as a navigational aid, you need to be careful, Devnee. Aryssa's best ability is studying the mirror."

Devnee did not want to be disloyal. "If I looked like that, I'd study the mirror, too." She dreamed that Trey answered with a shower of compliments: You do look like that, Dev! You'll give

Aryssa a run for her money! Till you moved here, Aryssa had no competition, but now! Whew!

Of course he didn't. He searched to find something about her that was interesting. "So where in town do you live, Devnee?"

Devnee told him.

He whistled without pitch. "The mansion at the bottom of the hill? Jeez. I knew the girl who used to live there. Creepy? Whew! I mean, that girl was creepy the way Aryssa is beautiful." He made a terrible face like he'd gag if he ran into that girl again.

Somebody behind them took part in the conversation. "Mega-creepy," said the person.

"Seriously creepy," added another.

"I was at that house for a party once," said Trey. He shuddered his shoulders on purpose. "Yeccchhh!"

"We're fixing up the house," said Devnee quickly. She did not want to be linked with some creepy girl who had made everybody gag. "We're going to paint it yellow to get rid of that dying mansion look."

"Take more than paint," muttered the voice from behind.

She thought of her shadow, of the cracks in the floor, and the shapes in the dark.

Yes. It would take more than paint.

"Here we are," said Trey. His face turned dark and threatening again. "English," he said regretfully. He studied Devnee for a minute. "I bet you're a real brain, huh?"

She flushed and shook her head. Trey figured someone as dumpy and dull as she was had to have something to offer. He was waiting to see it. He had a long wait.

English was her scariest subject. She was no student. She didn't mind reading homework, although it took her a long time, but she hated classroom reading. While the rest of the class flipped speedily along, page after page, she'd be slogging through the second paragraph. There were always pitying glances as the class tapped impatient fingers and waited for Devnee to catch up.

And in English, there were writing assignments. Devnee had a hard enough time putting her thoughts together inside her own head. To write them down was like being tossed in a cement mixer — upside down, head whacking against rotating walls.

If I talk out loud in English, thought Devnee, Trey will know I'm practically as dumb as Aryssa. But without the looks.

I wish I could look like that. But I wish I could be smart, too. If I were both beautiful *and* smart, what a wonderful life I would have!

This teacher was prepared to have a new student in the class; Fuzz had called ahead. Mrs. Cort had made a packet for Devnee of current readings and assignments. Mrs. Cort even said for Devnee not to worry about today or tomorrow, but just to concentrate on feeling at ease and finding her place.

What a nice, comforting smile Mrs. Cort had. And what a nice assignment: feeling at ease.

Devnee distracted herself thinking of smiles. Would she like a gorgeous, stunning smile like Aryssa? A tough, wrestling-partner smile like Trey? A kindly, neighborly smile like this teacher?

No contest.

Gorgeous and stunning. With a tough wrestling partner smiling back at her.

The class launched into a book discussion, and Devnee was surprised and delighted. Not only had her old school used the same curriculum — they'd been ahead! She had just finished reading the same book. What a gift! For several nights she would not have to do her English.

"We'll begin, please," said the teacher, "with a summary of the theories stated in the preface to the novel."

Everybody moaned. Devnee knew — because she had had this same class two weeks before in another state — that nobody ever read the preface.

A girl sitting one row ahead and one seat to the right, directly in Devnee's line of sight to the teacher, raised her hand.

"Yes, Victoria," said the teacher wearily, and Devnee knew instantly that Victoria was the kind of girl who always read, remembered, and analyzed the prefaces.

Victoria was a sort of reverse of Aryssa: a bold,

sweeping, athletic, rich beauty — a girl on a yacht, or on skis. A girl who skimmed the problems of life, laughing and full of energy. What a good name Victoria was for her.

As for her clothes, they were astonishing. Old corduroy pants, sagging socks, gaping shoes, coat-like sweater. It was clear that Victoria didn't care. Clothes were nothing to Victoria. She transcended clothing. What mattered to Victoria was exhibiting her brainpower.

She had a lot to exhibit.

Victoria more or less kept her hand up all period while the teacher looked around hopefully for somebody else to know at least one little fact, but nobody did, whereas Victoria always knew everything.

Devnee considered making a contribution. (In fact, it would be a quote from the smart kid in her last school, but who was to know?) However, Victoria also liked to argue, and Devnee was afraid she'd be in some academic argument on the first day of school, which she would certainly lose, so she said nothing.

The most surprising thing was that Victoria was interesting, even funny. It was a pleasure to listen to her comments, her unusual opinions, her scholarly jokes.

Devnee liked her immensely. She found herself smiling throughout the class, enjoying Victoria.

As Trey led the way to the cafeteria — it was

one of those interrupted classes; thirty minutes of class, twenty-five minutes of lunch, another twenty minutes of class — Devnee said, "Victoria seems like a nice person."

He grinned again. Grins seemed to come easily to him. "Hey, Vic!" he bellowed. "The new girl thinks you look like a nice person."

The class's roar of laughter filled the hall.

"Vic's smart," said one of the boys, "but nice? Ha!" But the boy was also smiling, both at Victoria and at Devnee. He, too, was handsome. Had she stumbled into a world where everybody else was a perfect physical specimen? Was she doomed to be a toad among princes and princesses?

"Nice," said Victoria, laughing, "is not a word we use very often around here. Nice is not the local specialty. But you do look like a nice person, Devnee. Have I pronounced it right? It's such an interesting name! Do you ever get called Dev?"

Victoria dropped back to link arms with Devnee. "I represent all scholarly talent in this building, Devnee. We have a very small brain pool."

Everybody was laughing.

"Now William here," she said, introducing the other perfect male specimen, "pretends to have brains. But no proof has yet emerged."

William smiled. "I'm the nice one," he promised Devnee, and this time nobody laughed, so it must have been true.

Everybody sat together for lunch; she was

jammed between Trey and Victoria. There were so many names revolving in Devnee's brain.

Trey took Devnee's tray back for her so she didn't have to clear her own place the first day. "You're too ladylike for this chore," he said to her, which prompted a fierce argument between him and Victoria on what made a lady, and whether such a creature existed, or should exist.

They went back to English at a trot; twenty-five minutes was barely enough time to stand in line, bolt down lunch, and make the return trip.

Devnee felt like taking a nap, or perhaps going back for another dessert, but Victoria, who had done extra reading, made pertinent comments about the author they were studying.

The class listened carefully. Devnee did not have the impression that anybody else was inspired to do extra reading, but they loved having Victoria around to be their brain, make great remarks, and know all the answers.

I wish I were as smart as that, thought Devnee. If I were as smart as Victoria, and as pretty as Aryssa . . .

Devnee drifted into a daydream of loveliness and intelligence.

In the dream she drew praise and applause, smiles and dates. In the dream she was the center of the room, just as Victoria was the center of this room, and Aryssa had been the center in the last one.

I'd like to be famous as well, thought Devnee. And rich, too. And very talented. Might as well have it all.

But she let go of the wishes to be famous and rich and talented. They were secondary.

Beauty was first. Then a mind. It would be so nice to have a mind that intrigued people.

Her third escort was Nina, a short-tempered girl who was obviously sorry she had volunteered. Nina kept glancing at her watch with the irritation of somebody who wants you to realize she has important things to do, and you're not one of them.

Nina never smiled. She never quite met Devnee's eyes, either, just glanced in the general direction of the new girl and set off. She didn't walk so they could walk next to each other, but she strode on ahead. She didn't glance back once to be sure Devnee was still trailing along. She waved to friends and called hello, but did not introduce Devnee.

Nina had fabulous clothes. The sweater definitely had cost more than Devnee could spend on an entire year's wardrobe.

When they reached class, Nina sat down and did not look at Devnee again. There was not an empty desk, and this teacher shared Nina's attitude; Devnee was a nuisance Mr. O'Sullivan could have done without. Devnee stood against the side wall, trying not to cry, trying to remember this was the same school where Mrs. Cort taught, and feeling at ease, and Victoria and Trey.

Finally a boy in the back row pushed his chair toward Devnee. It didn't reach her, so he kicked it again. It scraped on the floor, unwilling to travel toward Devnee. The class snickered. The boy kicked it a third time, and this time it sped over the floor and hit her in the kneecaps.

The boy lounged on top of his desk, legs swinging, expression cruel. Mr. O'Sullivan seemed amused. Devnee sat exposed on the chair, no desk in front to protect her, hands folded on her lap, as if she were praying, which she was.

When class finally ended, the boy launched himself off the desk like a rocket and vanished, while Nina took off with her friends. Devnee tagged after them, afraid of this huge school, these many floors and wings and courtyards. "Nina?" Devnee said nervously. "Can you show me how to get out?"

Nina stared at her, repelled, as if finding a raw clam on her peanut butter sandwich. "How to get out?" repeated Nina, arching her eyebrows. "I suggest a door." Nina and her friends laughed and walked on.

Devnee forced herself to laugh, also. "I mean, the school is so big and I don't exactly know where the front entrance is. Where my mother is picking me up."

"Your mother is picking you up?" said Nina, as if normal people stopped having mothers when they left elementary school. "You don't have your own car?" Nina's eyebrows went up again. Her friends imitated her.

Their scorn filled the halls.

Devnee hated them.

Nina sniffed, making a big deal of Devnee being in her way. "Trey!" Nina yelled down the hall. "Hey, Trey! Show the new girl where the front hall is, will you? *I'm* not taking that much of a detour."

Trey had a bookbag on his back and an athletic bag in each hand. He was with William, who was similarly burdened, clearly heading for the gym and some sport or other. "Sure, be glad to," said Trey.

"Come with us, Dev," added William.

"You don't have to take me," Devnee said quickly. "It's out of your way. Just point me in the right direction."

"The right direction includes several turns and two different stairs. Don't worry about it. And don't worry about Nina, either. She doesn't exactly have the greatest personality in the world." William's smile was like Mrs. Cort's, as easy and kind as a backyard swing.

"She does have the greatest car, though," said Trey.

"Does she ever," agreed William. "What I wouldn't give to be as rich as she is."

"How rich is she, Bill?" asked Devnee.

William stopped dead, sneakers squeaking. He dropped his gym bag. "I'm William. No nicknames. Let's get this relationship started out right. William, okay?"

I can't even talk right, she thought. She wanted to start crying right then, but tears would drive them off forever. Her father was right; no one could stand a whiner. "William. Okay."

They shook on it. Her hand was sweaty and damp, and his was strong and smooth.

"Nina," said William, answering the question, "could probably buy and sell the town."

Devnee would settle for the sweater. And palms that did not sweat.

Trey and William not only took her to the door, but right on out to the car, where her mother sat with the engine idling.

"See you tomorrow, Devnee," said Trey.

"Thanks so much, Trey," she said, turning to wave good-bye. "Nice to meet you, William."

Behind the two boys, the school loomed large and solid, red bricks glowing in the afternoon sun. As the boys charged back into the building to get to practice on time, Devnee's shadow slipped out the school door, rushing to catch up.

Nobody else saw it.

A slip of black, coasting on a sidewalk.

Quivers of sickness climbed up her throat like a scream. *Why weren't you with me? I can't be a person without a shadow!*

"So how was school?" said her mother happily. "My day was wonderful. Wait till you see all I've accomplished!"

Devnee held the door open, and her shadow got in the car and disappeared against the upholstery.

Chapter 4

That night, the tower was ordinary.

The hours of darkness passed serenely.

She slept well.

In the morning, the sun smiled, the snow glittered, and the sky was pure. School was perfect. It was too soon to have friends, but everybody was friendly. Trey and Aryssa, William and Victoria and all the rest — what a fine school this was! What a fine life she was entering!

Only that last period, with Mr. O'Sullivan's sneer and Nina's contempt, was difficult. He did not order another desk, and Devnee remained exposed on the chair, taking notes on her lap. But now she knew the school well enough to run down the hall alone when class ended, catch Trey and William, and be escorted to her car by two laughing handsome boys.

Over the weekend she went shopping with her mother, looking for clothes similar to what Aryssa wore. (Nobody would want to dress like Victoria, and nobody could afford to dress like Nina.) It was one of those wonderful shopping expeditions when everything fit, every price was right, every style was flattering. Devnee spun home, twirling in delight.

Her father and brother had been at work in the tower.

The interior shutters had been opened and fastened by the strangely heavy, prisonlike clasps. "One window was broken, Devnee," said her father. "I just reglazed it, and your brother and I washed the windows inside and out. I hung on to Luke's knees while he sat on the sill to do the outside. He also fixed the banging shutter on the outside."

"Hey, great," said Devnee. How airy, how bright the room was! A special room for a special person. A room for giggling friends and silly slumber parties. Devnee danced. Her father went downstairs with the tools.

Luke stayed in the tower, a strange expression on his face. He started to laugh but it turned into a croak. Started to shrug, but twitched instead. Started to talk, but mumbled incoherently.

"Luke, you're so worthless," said Devnee with a sisterly laugh.

"I think you should take the downstairs bedroom after all," he said.

"What? You bum! You want the tower now, huh? You think just because you washed a window you get the tower? Forget it."

"No! I want —" He broke off. He looked around

him, as if thinking they would be overheard and punished. He whispered, "I want you to be all right."

For a moment her heart crashed, her hands iced. She remembered her shadow, the slimy touch in the night, the breathing room in the dark. What had Luke felt up here, touching those shutter slats where her shadow's long black fingers had explored? What did Luke know, from this creepy room that knew all the secrets of night?

"Place is spooky," muttered Luke. He headed for the stairs. His movement broke the spell.

My own stairs, thought Devnee, laughing again. Wait'll I have Aryssa over. Will she ever be impressed! "Honestly, Luke," she said. "I have a chance to be happy and you try to make things up to scare me."

"I'm not making anything up. And the least you could do is thank me for fixing your stupid window. I hate having a sister."

"Well, I hate having a brother. Get out of here."

"Not till you say thank you!"

"Thank you. Now get out. I want to try on my new clothes."

He was almost down the stairs when he turned to look at her. His body was no longer visible, only his head. Decapitated, the lips moved anyway. Devnee shuddered, and a hand ran gently over her back, and stroked her neck under her hair. She whirled to face it, but of course there was nobody there.

"You deserve whatever you get," said Luke. "So there."

The next Thursday, Devnee was late to school. She had to spend a few minutes in the office getting yelled at and being marked Present after all. The secretary seemed to feel that if you were going to be late, you should just be absent, and save everybody the trouble of reentering you in the day's computer list. Devnee didn't mind. She loved this school now, and could even love a sulky, short-tempered secretary.

She was happy within these walls.

As for nights in the tower and shadows at her feet, she could only assume that the first day in a new town had scared her so badly she'd given herself bad dreams.

Devnee gathered her things and went slowly down the hall.

Was she lucky that her new down jacket was so slippery it slid from her grasp? Was she lucky that she had to kneel and scoop it up with her two free fingers, then try to stagger to her feet without also dropping six books, homework, and chorus folder? Was she lucky that everything slid onto the floor a second time, so she remained bent like a clumsy acolyte kneeling in front of a school altar?

Kneeling like a beggar or a slave, Devnee heard two voices.

Just around the corner, laughing and low, each

voice had a rich texture. Talking between classes —
telling secrets — had thickened the voices. But
they were not so thick that Devnee failed to recognize them.

"She's absent today!" said the first voice.
Aryssa's voice. From the throat of velvet and the
lips of red. "What a relief."

"I know," said the second voice. Trey's voice. "If I
have to waste time with her much longer, I'm going to puke."

Devnee's knees crunched on the floor. Her new
clothes did not seem so pretty, nor her jacket so
trendy.

"The trouble with the buddy system," said the
first voice, "is that they really think you're their
buddy." It was Aryssa.

Dread clamped down on Devnee's joy. I don't
want to hear this, she thought. Go away. Don't say
it out loud. I can guess now. Don't make me know
the truth. Please. Let me pretend I'm pretty and
nice.

"That's the trouble with being friendly," Aryssa
went on. "You can't just be friendly. You end up
with this person who thinks she's really your
friend." Aryssa laughed.

Trey clucked sympathetically. "There's nothing
really wrong with Devnee," he said. "We'll let her
tag along for a while. Eventually she'll make real
friends and drift off."

"No," said Aryssa, "I know that kind. She never
catches on. She never picks up a clue. She'll be

there forever. You'd have to run over her with a truck to convince her you don't want her around."

Trey laughed. "Why did you volunteer to be her buddy anyway?" he asked.

"Because I'm failing biology again," said Aryssa. "She looked smart and I figured she could do my labs for me and during tests I could crib off her. But she turned out to be just as dumb as I am. You should see us in bio lab, Trey. We're pathetic."

Trey laughed. "*She's* pathetic," he said. "You're beautiful."

Aryssa laughed. "Thank you, darling." There was a smoochy sound.

Devnee was gripping her books so hard she broke a fingernail.

"Why did *you* volunteer?" asked Aryssa.

"You know why. I wanted to make time with Victoria, and Victoria approves of being decent to the pitiful ones. Victoria's very big on charity. Look how Victoria is sitting with Devnee at lunch." There was another smoochy sound. "But Victoria doesn't matter now, either, does she?" said Trey, and he and Aryssa laughed together.

Devnee was still crouched over her belongings. One of the pitiful ones to whom Victoria felt people should be charitable.

If Trey and Aryssa came this way, they would find her, like a dog outside its kennel, waiting to be kicked.

But they walked in the other direction. Trey's

heavy shoes and Aryssa's delicate heels played a duet on the hard cold tiles. And Devnee Fountain remained a solo, as she had always been, without friends, without beauty, without hope.

The strange thing was that Devnee did not hate them.

Instead she felt guilty for being a burden. They were beautiful people, interesting people, and they were right: She had attached herself like a poison ivy vine to a tree. Of course they didn't want her there. She was giving them a rash.

I was born plain, she thought, and Luke is right. I deserve whatever I get. I had daydreams too big. I wanted to be happy, and pretty, and popular. Instead I was a nuisance and made Trey want to puke.

So after biology lab, Devnee said to Aryssa, "You've been a great buddy, Aryssa. But I'm pretty well oriented now. I'll be okay."

Aryssa gave the incredibly sweet smile that had so impressed Devnee the first day. This was the gift Aryssa wanted, not friendship, not company, not a slumber party in a tower — but freedom from the burden of Devnee. "You're so darling, Dev," Aryssa said.

Devnee could not speak another syllable. Her voice would break. She nodded. Aryssa smiled again, like an archangel, like a star in the heavens, and danced over to her real friends.

How final the passage was.

How complete the end of Devnee's plans for a new life in a new school.

Devnee knew that her heart had still been hoping. Her heart had beaten on, telling itself that Aryssa would answer, "Nonsense, Devnee, we're *real* buddies, you and I; I'm so glad you moved here!"

Her heart was a fool.

Devnee stood alone, without a buddy, in the door of biology lab, and saw that Aryssa was not the only beautiful girl. She was part of a crowd of beautiful girls; a page full of magazine models, haughty and perfect.

Now she knew they had been laughing at her all along.

"Hey, buddy," said Trey cheerfully.

Her heart dissolved this time; she had an acid bath in her chest. She said bravely, "Thanks for being my buddy, Trey. I'll be fine on my own now."

"Hey, great," said Trey. He knotted his big hand into a friendly fist and gave her a friendly tap on the shoulder.

I want a kiss and a hug, she thought, and I'm getting a clenched-fist good-bye.

"You're a very well-adjusted person, you know that?" said Trey. "I mean, you settled in really well, Devnee." He, too, left to be with his real friends, with handsome William and the others. "You take care of yourself now, Devnee," he called back, as if he would never see her again.

And he did not.

In the days that followed, Trey, who was in two classes with her, plus lunch, never saw her again. He moved in his crowd, the beautiful crowd, and Devnee blended into the ordinary group, the ones on whom Trey's eyes would never focus and with whom Aryssa would never laugh.

The only person who continued to be a friend was Victoria. Victoria, who told her potential boyfriends they had to be nice to losers, or Victoria wouldn't be nice to them.

I'm a loser! thought Devnee. She perfected the art of tilting her head back to keep the tears from rolling down her cheeks.

If only I were beautiful! Oh, how I wish I could be beautiful!

Chapter 5

The school bus drove down the long slow hill. Even the road seemed reluctant to get to the bottom where Devnee's mansion lay among the dark and angry evergreens. The road was filled with little rises, as if trying to escape arriving in the valley.

From the school bus window, she could see the many-angled roof, the tall chimneys and the tower.

There was no sun, of course; it was not a day for sun. And yet the windows of the tower gleamed, and spoke to her, and called her name.

The bus stopped.

Only Devnee got off.

Nobody said good-bye.

Nobody watched her go.

Nobody saw that her shadow went first.

The shadow waited for Devnee to catch up, and Devnee knew that they were going to the tower together. She knew that the tower was waiting for them both. The tower knew things she did not. Could not. Should not.

She was oddly excited.

Her scalp prickled but she did not shrink from it.

She felt that perhaps her personality had split, just as her shadow and body had split. She was going to be two people in this town: a tower person and a school person.

"How was school?" her mother asked gaily. Her mother was so involved in kitchen remodeling, so happy choosing faucet styles and cabinet knobs that she thought everybody was just as happy.

"Pretty good." Devnee could not even remember the happiness of last week.

"Oh, darling, I know we made the right decision moving to this town and buying this house!"

Devnee had difficulty getting warm. The winter dampness had entered her bones, her lungs, even her heart. She put a kettle on the stove, heating water over the gas burner instead of sticking a mug in the microwave, just to get heat from the tiny blue flames. The flames curled away from her, as if even they found her too dull and plain to even heat water for.

The house creaked and groaned. During supper, her father got up twice to see where the draft was coming from, to shut a door here and check a window there.

Devnee's dreams from the first night crept up her back and lodged against her neck. Something dark and cold, something of ink and something of fungus crawled over her skin.

"I'm rotting," she said out loud. "I have nothing to offer, and my body knows it, and it's rotting."

Her father gave her his most irritated look.

Luke gave her his "why is this my sister?" look.

Her mother of course ignored the statement. Her mother hated being reminded of how dull, how ordinary her daughter was. Instead her mother said, "Now don't let this old house worry you, sweet pea. The house does make eerie noises, but it's just an old-fashioned heating system warming up and cooling off. Why, soon it'll feel as if you always lived here."

Perhaps I always have, thought Devnee. My shadow already knows every room; my shadow has been here before. My shadow will stay here after I am gone.

She went to bed early.

The tower was even colder than the rest of the house.

She was not surprised when her shadow peeled away, when it crossed the tower room. Cautiously, as if testing the waters.

When Devnee turned out the light, her shadow did not evaporate. It became a darker dark than the rest of the room.

Her soul darkened with it, and all her hatreds and jealousies filled the spaces of the tower, crowding against the walls, against the windows. Through the crowded anger, the packed despair, came a voice, as liquid as oozing mud.

The voice sounded trapped, condensed, under-water. It sounded heavy and drowning.

Devnee could not understand the words. Perhaps they were not words, but rumblings from ancient history.

Devnee Fountain got out of bed, holding her hands in front of her to feel her way through the dark, trying to find the voice.

Her shadow wrapped itself around her legs, hanging on to her. Pushing her back toward the bed. She kicked the air to free herself from the clinging shadow. This is how Aryssa felt toward me, she thought. I was nothing but dark air to her, to be kicked off at the end of the week.

Devnee was wearing a long flannel nightgown, because it was cold in the old house. Icy drafts crept between every crack. The nightgown caught between her feet, and tripped her. As she tumbled to the floor, the cracks in the wood widened as if the tower were having an earthquake. She cried out and clutched the wall to keep herself from falling into a crack. It opened as wide as a crevasse in Antarctica, to swallow a dog team or a downed plane, and she found a handle on the wall and held it.

She was suffocating.

She was hot and her head was throbbing from tower thoughts. Her shadow — her shadow was coming off — but not by choice — it —

— was being torn off.

There was no pain, but a severing. She had been amputated.

The shadow had not chosen to go.

The shadow had been taken.

I have to have air, thought Devnee, and flung open the window.

Wind screamed into the tower as if it had been bottled for years. The pressure of its arrival knocked her back into the center of the room, and the room felt huge, as if she could run backward for days and not hit the other wall.

She might have opened her heart as well as the window. Body and soul were exposed, more painfully than even in Mr. O'Sullivan's room. With every breath, her lungs ached in the bitter wind.

A piece of darkness became solid, and she caught it, thinking it was her shadow. It wrapped around her.

Velvet, lined with slime.

Not her shadow.

It was the answer to her wish.

Devnee could not quite see the answer.

It — he — floated in and out of focus like a distant mirage far down a highway.

He came from the cracks in the shutters, and he remained attached to them, legless. His cloak drifted toward her and shifted back, the way sea anemones did in the aquarium, tentacles rising and falling with the tide. His cloak rose and fell with her breathing, as if she had become his lungs.

Together they breathed in the tower air.

Together they studied each other.

She could not see his body, although she was aware of it, glowing and phosphorescent behind the desk. His face was visible only when the cloak was not weaving in front of it.

His eyes glittered like ice cubes. His teeth were like frozen, sharpened milk. His lips were stretched like pale rubber bands.

She wanted to run, but she wanted to be part of him and know him.

Her shadow embroidered the dark, stitching itself in the corners and darting past the shutters.

The dark drapery of his garments shifted and swirled and the hem blew toward Devnee's fingers. In a voice as sticky as spiderwebs, he said, "Touch it."

She shook her head.

How could it be so dark, so black and midnight, and yet she continued to see? Dark had become light, and the darkness of him made a path.

"Yes," he said. His voice purred. "A path. It will take us both where we want to go. I think I heard you make a wish, my dear. A wish. I came for your wish."

A wish? She could not remember wishing for anything. Except the impossible. Beauty. Friends. Fun.

The cloak stroked her hand.

She whimpered and yanked the hand back, but

the cloak arranged itself into fingers and tightened its grip. Chill surrounded her ankles like a damp moldy blanket. She could not move or think.

"Wish on it," he breathed.

She wanted to put her other hand down and peel away the cloak. But what if it caught both her hands? Where would she go then? How would she get free?

"You wished, I think," came the voice, as rich and comforting as melted chocolate, "for Beauty."

Aryssa entered her mind, as clear and devastatingly beautiful as a portrait in a gallery.

If you possessed Beauty, the rest came of its own accord. Beautiful girls stayed gracefully in one place, while along came Fame, and Riches, and Friends. If you had Beauty, people loved to look at you; and the longer they looked at you, the more they fell in love with you. If you had Beauty, there was nothing you could not do: no problem you could not conquer, no pain you could not assuage.

For a dark moment she tasted Beauty, and all that it could mean. Then her shadow swept down around her and touched her feet. For a moment she felt normal.

The shadow pressed closer, and she knew this was what her shadow wanted. She took a step back, and the cloak fell from her hand, the wind lessened, and the chill evaporated. Devnee took another step back and felt for the wall switch. The shadow clung to her arm, coaxing her back to bed.

"If, my dear," he said, "if you were beautiful . . ."

He covered his mouth and smiled behind his hands. His fingers were all bone and no flesh.

She was shocked. "You must be starving," she said.

"Yes." The *ssss* of the word lasted a long time, singing in her ears, deafening her. "I am starving," he agreed. "That is *my* wish, Devnee Fountain. Something to feed upon. Perhaps, my dear, we could trade wishes. I will give you mine, and you will give me yours."

She tried to think about this, but the *ssss* of his *yessssss* curled around her and seeped into her ears and her eyes and her thoughts, and confused her.

"What is your wisssssshhhh?" he whispered.

The *ssssshhhh* floated through her brain, and she said firmly, "I want it all."

Now he laughed. It was the sound of breaking glass. "Nobody has it all, my dear."

"But they do. On TV all the time you see somebody who has it all. And in school, lots of girls have it all."

"Name one."

"Aryssa."

"She has only beauty."

"It's enough," said Devnee. "She has everything because she has beauty. If I had beauty . . ." I would have buddies who really love me, she thought. I would link arms and make phone calls and have fun. All it takes is to be beautiful, but I was born plain and I will never have a chance to be anything else. "Still," she said, "I want it all."

"That is a thousand wishes. You must start with one. Gradually you will collect it all, my dear. I promise you that in exchange. But you must choose the place to start."

Wishes were important to Devnee. Whether she wished on a birthday candle, or a wishbone, or the first star of the evening, she really pondered her wish, to be sure she wished right, that there were no hitches, that it really was her first choice.

"Aryssa," he repeated. "Such a lovely name. Such a lovely girl."

Yes, thought Devnee. Such a lovely girl. That dark hair, such a perfect cut. That fair face, such a lovely form. Those sweet soft eyes so deep beneath her brow. Her walk, like a dancer lingering with her partner.

His cape flew back and tightened around him, celebrating something. "What a wonderful description!" he breathed. "Yes, definitely the right choice."

Devnee looked at him uneasily. "I didn't say anything out loud."

"You don't need to," he said. "I am in your mind."

She shuddered. Her shadow trembled. "Give me back that thought," she said. "It's mine."

"No. You are in my tower. And I am in your head and heart." How brittle the laugh was. How desperate. What was it that he wanted? And how could she, Devnee Fountain, give it to him?

"Aryssa is not a very nice person, is she?" he

went on. "Should a mean, small-minded person like her be allowed to have such beauty?"

Devnee stood very still.

"While a gentle, kind, hardworking person like you, is . . . well . . . perhaps . . . a little less beautiful?"

"I'm plain," she said. She found herself holding Aryssa responsible for this. How dare Aryssa be born so perfect?

"Plain. A dreadful word," he sympathized. "Nobody wants to be plain. I know how you wish you were beautiful."

She nodded.

"I love wishes," he said. "I have one myself."

She was bending toward him. Her shadow was bending away.

"Make a wish," he breathed.

Devnee caught the edge of the cape. For one sick, dizzy moment she felt as if she were holding the edge of a swamp, a pond full of poison. A queer stench rose up and she tried to turn away, tried to catch a breath of fresh air. The tower seemed close and fetid, as if something there were rotting in those terrible cracks that opened by night.

"Make a wish!" He drooled over the words. His trunk pulsed back and forth, as if he were on a spring. He isn't a ghost, she thought. He has too much form. And he is too dark.

She wanted to run downstairs to the kitchen full of sawdust and paper plates and family laughter.

He said, "Here's my offer."

I have to get out of here, thought Devnee. She managed to focus her eyes, managed to find her shadow, managed with her eyes to draw it back to herself. Its thin presence snuggled weakly against her.

"You want to be beautiful?" he said. "I will give you Aryssa's beauty."

Have Aryssa's beauty! Imagine that. Imagine waking up in the morning, looking in your mirror, and seeing Aryssa there! Imagine how the boys would admire; how the girls would envy!

Aryssa's beauty.

"But what about Aryssa?"

"What about her?"

"What will she have?"

He smiled. The teeth were immense and sharp and dripping with slime. "What she deserves," he said.

Oh, what a wonderful thought — that people got what they deserved! Yes! Aryssa should get what she deserved. Aryssa and Trey, saying that being buddies with Devnee made them puke! She would show them! They wouldn't say that again in a hurry!

"I wish I were beautiful," cried Devnee Fountain. "I wish I looked like Aryssa."

The cape jerked free, rasping over her skin, as painful as a handful of paper cuts. The cape wrapped itself around him like a container. Just before he vanished, she saw how his teeth overhung his lower lip, sharp as a row of garden stakes.

He was a vampire.

In that dark and terrible moment, Devnee Fountain knew what would happen to Aryssa.

But she did nothing. She did not take back her wish. Hot revenge filled her mind, ugly as a hundred vampires.

Aryssa would get what she deserved.

Devnee smiled, and the smile was sharp, and cruel.

Her shadow did not come back.

Chapter 6

In school they liked you to think. Thinking carefully and logically was a reason for school. You got graded on your thinking and Devnee tended to think more inside the building than out of it.

Today, however, Devnee Fountain sat, carefully *not* thinking.

Not thinking took a lot of energy. It required concentration far beyond mere thinking. *Not* thinking meant taking complete control of her mind and eyes and daydreams.

Not thinking required Devnee to split her personality and allot some to the teacher, some to the paper, some to the human beings around her, and none whatsoever, not a whisper, not a glimmer, to last night.

Last night.

It crept into her mind even as she fought its memory.

She saw it, smelled it, tasted it, felt it, and most of all . . . heard it.

"You see," he had whispered, *"I cannot get anything for myself. It must be given to me. And so I offer you, my dear, a fair exchange."*

His voice echoed. It did not stay where it belonged, twelve hours before. It spread like spilled oil on a pond, its dark sticky slime rimming the edges of her soul.

Her wish.

It was there. She could have it. She could take it.

It required only Aryssa.

In biology lab they were still partners. Aryssa still did not want to touch anything, and especially not today, when they had progressed to an eyeball. It came from a cow, said the teacher, and today they would —

Aryssa covered her ears and squinted her eyes shut. "You do it, Devnee," ordered Aryssa.

Devnee did not look at Aryssa. She looked at the rest of the biology lab class. Nobody wanted to look down at the metal dissection tray, and several people had chosen to look at Aryssa instead. Girls looked at Aryssa with a sort of distant longing. Boys looked at Aryssa in admiration mixed with a much closer longing, a longing called desire.

The girls wanted to look like Aryssa, but the boys wanted to have her.

If I looked like Aryssa . . . thought Devnee.

And *last night* he said, *"But you can! So easily!"*

Devnee, too, shut her eyes and winced, but it was not because of the eyeball. It was because of a certain darkness out in the school yard, a long straight glimmering path of . . . *him.*

Aryssa was too curious and eventually had to look down. She literally gagged, put her hand over her mouth, and swallowed hard. Then she went white, panting and acting faint.

"Are you all right, Aryssa?" said the boys solicitously. "Devnee, do it for her."

"Are you all right, Aryssa?" said the teacher gently. "Take a deep breath and that will help you pull together."

"Are you all right, Aryssa?" said the girls. "Devnee, she can't do that kind of thing. You're her buddy. You do it."

Aryssa managed not to throw up or pass out. She patted Devnee's knee. "I'm glad I have you, Devnee. It's so nice to have a buddy."

The eyeball before them was immense, as if it were several eyes rolled together. Its texture was both jellylike and rocklike. The rest of the class gripped and dug in. The room was noisy with the squeals of horrified girls and the grunts of sickened boys. The room was definitely on an equal opportunity basis when it came to being squeamish.

Devnee looked at Aryssa's lovely fragile face, her gentle mouth, her sweet eyes, her hair flowing like a dark and shining river.

"If I dissect it for you," said Devnee, her voice and her resolve faltering, "what will you do for me?" She was horrified to hear her voice break, hear herself begging. She might as well be on her knees.

She might as well be weeping. *Be my buddy. Like me. Sit with me because you enjoy my company. Say something nice to me! Please!*

Aryssa was amazed. Me, do something for you? her eyebrows said.

Surely Devnee was joking. The equation did not go both ways.

I want friendship even more than beauty, Devnee realized suddenly, and she almost decided against beauty; she almost waited for the next night, to explain to him that —

But then she thought: None of these people really like Aryssa anyway. It's her beauty they like. They don't want her to faint or throw up because she wouldn't be beautiful anymore. She wouldn't be something for them to adore.

She tried to sort out what was beauty and what was friendship but they were running out of time.

"Girls," said the teacher sharply.

Devnee looked up guiltily.

Aryssa opened her eyes to see that Devnee was not dissecting, either. "Come on, Devnee," she said impatiently. "Do it."

A queer sick thrill ran through Devnee.

Aryssa had just chosen her future. Aryssa had just given permission.

Aryssa had just made a very serious mistake.

"All right," said Devnee. The thrill ripped through her, like some weird electrical charge that did not kill, but energized. Devnee's eyes were very wide, they felt as large as the cows' eyes; they felt as if they would burst. How clearly she could see the dark path now.

She got up off her high lab stool.

She did not even blink. She felt less human, as if no bodily functions were going on, no blinking, no digesting, no breathing, no pumping.

She was all desire.

She was all choice.

She knew where she was going, and she did not care.

She was going to be beautiful.

For a moment she stumbled, as something was wrenched away, and she looked around in surprise, and almost in anger, but nobody had touched her and nobody had seen anything.

Only her shadow. It had pulled loose again.

Her shadow would attach itself only to a human, and what Devnee was going to do was not human.

For a moment she let herself think. For a moment the thoughts — terrible, shameful, evil thoughts — circulated in her brain.

But nobody was paying any attention to her. Even the teacher did not care that Devnee was walking to the back of the room instead of working. Even Aryssa had lost interest. Devnee Fountain was not worth the effort of tracking.

In the rear of the classroom, Devnee opened a window.

A shaft came through. Not light. Not as if the sun had suddenly come out. But as if the dark had suddenly come in.

It lay vibrating, that path.

Devnee went back to her stool. She picked up her scalpel. "If you want, Aryssa, you can stand over there at the back of the room till I've finished up."

The eyeball looked right through Devnee, into her heart. It saw what she was doing, and how.

She carefully did not think. If she thought, she would know. If she knew, she would stop. So it was best neither to think nor to know.

Aryssa slipped off her high stool and drifted to the back of the room.

The teacher said with a frown, "Aryssa?"

"I have to get a sip of water," explained Aryssa, giving the teacher her meltingly beautiful smile, and getting the usual melting response.

The eyeball stared on.

Devnee put a scalpel through it.

The tower was dark, and she did not bother to turn on the light. He was more likely to come in the dark anyhow. It was a matter of waiting. She waited a long time.

She wondered what he was doing all that time.

All night long.

When he came, it was almost dawn. At first he was quite hard to see: He was all oozing cape and wrinkled foil fingernails.

And then he smiled.

She had never seen him smile before.

His teeth were immense as posters on walls, dripping blades.

Dripping blood.

Devnee gasped. "What —" she whispered.

"What did you think?" the vampire said.

"I thought — "

"You knew," said the vampire calmly.

"I —" Devnee staggered backward. "I thought you were — like — a visitor — or — a — night creature — or — like — a dark ghost."

The vampire laughed. He sounded rich and contented, like cream soup.

She cried, "I thought you would — like — haunt her!"

"Now, Devnee. You knew what I would do. You saw the tools of my trade. You counted the hours of night in which I was busy."

This night — this night in which she had done her homework, and written up her lab experiment, and argued with her brother, and had an extra snack — this night he had . . . the vampire had . . . Aryssa had . . .

She could not think about it.

It was not decent to think about things like that.

"It was a good trade," he told her. "You got Aryssa's beauty, and I got —" He smiled again. He dried his teeth on his cape, and once more they gleamed white, shimmering like sharpened pearls.

Now she knew why the cape was dark and crusted, and why it stank of swamps and rot.

Devnee licked her lips and wished she hadn't. She clung to the shutters for strength and wished she hadn't. At last she said, "But what happened?"

"What do you think, my dear?"

"I'm trying not to think," said Devnee.

"Ah yes. You humans are very good at that. It's probably for the best, Devnee, my dear. And of course, a beautiful girl does not need to think. And now you are beautiful." His eyebrows arched like cathedral doorways, thin and pointing, vanishing beneath his straight black hair. With his eyebrows up, his eyes seemed much wider. Too wide. As if they were from biology lab. As if they were half dissected.

"Is Aryssa — is she — I mean — will she — that is —"

"She'll be fine," said the vampire. "She's just rather tired right now. She won't be in school much for the next few weeks. And of course when she does come back, she'll be plain. Nobody will notice her. The way it was for you. But that's all right, isn't it, Devnee Fountain? You thought it quite a reasonable exchange, didn't you, Devnee Fountain?"

"Don't call me by both my names," she said to him.

"Why? Does it make everything too real?" He laughed drowsily. He rocked back and forth contentedly.

Devnee tried not to think about that.

Actually, he did look healthier. His skin, usually the color of mushrooms, had a pinkish tinge. As if for the first time blood circulated in his body.

"What about my shadow?" said Devnee.

The vampire blinked. Frowned. The eyebrows

landed and sat heavily over his eyes, as if keeping them from falling out as he rocked. "Your shadow?"

"It keeps on separating from me."

The vampire's smile was slow and pleased; his lips spread like drapery over a dark window. Teeth hung over the narrow lips like foam on a sea wave. "It does, doesn't it?" he said dreamily. "Shadows," said the vampire, separating the words in a cruel, bored way, "shadows . . . prefer not . . . to be present . . . when the . . ." He smiled again. ". . . when the event . . . occurs."

"Event?" said Devnee. She was very cold. Her skin felt slick, as if she were growing mold. Or as if the vampire's mold was migrating and attaching itself to her flesh. She wrapped the quilt more tightly around herself, pulling its hem up around her neck, until she was hooded in a comforter. It did not comfort her.

Especially when the vampire touched her cheek. She flinched and jumped backward.

"Shadows love the dark. I am the dark. Your shadow needed, as you say in this century, to make contact."

She heard a noise outside the tower. The wind increased and came through the closed windows as it had before, and the chill was greater and the mold colder.

"Morning," said the vampire.

He sifted back through the slits of the shutters, into the vanishing night.

"What are you made of?" said Devnee.

"Shadows," he said. "Victims of many centuries. Collected in one cape. Under one set of teeth, as it were. I am thick with the shadows of the dead."

"Aryssa?" cried Devnee. "I thought — *she isn't dead, is she?* I thought you — I thought I —"

"She's not beautiful anymore," said the vampire. "She might as well be dead. Isn't that what *you* told me?"

He was all gone except his fingernails, wrapped around the final slat.

But his voice continued on. A separate funnel of sound and horror.

"Sweet dreams, Devnee," his voice said.

And his laughter curled into the dawn, his dark path retreated and, after a long time, Devnee Fountain turned around and went to find a mirror.

Chapter 7

She paused without looking in front of her own mirror in the tower. Anything in the tower was suspect, could be corrupted. She kept her eyes lowered. She needed a real mirror, one that would not lie.

How strange, thought Devnee. My lashes feel longer. I can feel them against my cheeks.

She went down the tower stairs to the second floor. There was no need to turn on the light. The dark path lit a way for her. It caressed her ankles and spread a velvet carpet to escort her down.

But the bathroom she shared with Luke was also uncertain. It knew her. She needed a pure, untouched mirror.

Down the final flight of stairs she went. Into the wide hallway with its wallpaper half stripped off. Back toward the kitchen, past the debris of remodeling, the tiles torn off, the lights dangling by wires. She could see as clearly as if it were noon. Through the pantry she went, to the powder room door.

The heavy dark wood of the bathroom door was not flat, like her tower door or the bedroom doors. It had panels of wood, making a raised T. Or a cross. She smiled at the cross. The vampire had not entered this bathroom. This mirror was of the world.

Devnee took a deep breath. She turned the handle. There was no need to step in. The mirror faced the door.

She lifted her lashes and looked at her reflection.

A beautiful girl looked back.

A girl whose dark hair was not lank and dull, but clouds of curling wisps.

A girl whose complexion was not pale and worn, but as fair as springtime, tinged with bright pink energy.

A girl whose eyes were not tired as dishwater, but whose eyes laughed and sparkled, and whose lashes swept mysteries before them.

Devnee laughed, and the new face laughed with her, teasing and coaxing and adorable.

Devnee raised her eyebrows and the new eyebrows were both comic and inviting.

Devnee thought deeply, and the face turned sober and gentle and full of compassion.

I am beautiful.

I have it. I have beauty.

I am not Aryssa. I do not look like her. And yet I have what she has: I have beauty. I have what makes people stop and stare. I have what makes people yearn and love.

I am Devnee Fountain.

I am beautiful.

She stood for a long time facing the mirror; stood, in fact, until dawn had come, and alarm clocks had gone off, and the rest of her family was stumbling into wakefulness.

Devnee, too, awoke.

But there was no stumbling now. No early morning heaviness. No dull resignation about yet another difficult school day ahead.

Tingling with excitement, she danced to the bathroom she shared with Luke, and wonder of wonders, he was still asleep. The floor was not covered with wet towels, and the soap was not lying in a disgusting soppy puddle at the bottom of the tub.

She felt thinner and more graceful.

The water showered down on her as if it were a privilege.

When she stepped out and wrapped herself in a towel, she tugged the pale blue plastic shower cap off and let her hair fall around her shoulders. In the foggy mirror of the hot bathroom, she looked at her reflection.

Clouds of hair, curly with humidity, wafted around her face like a bridal veil.

That's what I am, she thought. A bride. Today I go to school for the first time with the veil lifted. I used to be covered by a plain dull boring face and body, but now I am what I deserve to be.

Beautiful.

Even my brother wished this for me, she thought, laughing with wild delight. I hope you get what you deserve, he had said, and I have! Her exuberance rose up in her like a storm of fireworks, celebrating from the inside out. She wanted to scream and shout and drive through town honking a horn. Look at me! I am beautiful!

She corralled her exuberance. It would not do. She must look as if she had always looked this way.

The girl in the mirror was still Devnee, but both sharpened and softened. Nature had not quite come through for Devnee at birth, but the essential elements of Devnee's features had been good, and now because of last night she had been brought into perfection.

Devnee stroked the reflection in the mirror, and even with the fog wiped off the glass, she remained beautiful. She was not a cloud. Not a mirage. She was real, and she was beautiful.

Luke began pounding on the door. "Get outta there, Dev!" her brother bellowed. "You think you're the only one living here?"

For a moment the insides of her — the person who had not changed — the person who was still the old Devnee — was thrown.

Who *was* living here?

She stared at the mirror and instead of being thrilled, she was terrified and confused. *Who is that?* Pieces of Aryssa, pasted together? Leftover victims of the vampire, summoned from the grave to be reflected in a mirror?

Where did the old Devnee go? Who is Aryssa now? Where is Aryssa now? Is Aryssa all right? What *did* happen last night?

Is this beauty only in my mind? What if the vampire just convinced me there was a trade?

Devnee opened the door before Luke smashed his way in.

Her yucky worthless brother paused in the doorway. A glare remained suspended on his face. The face itself became confused. Her brother was staring at her with awe.

"Gosh, Sis," he said. "You look great. I like your hair like that."

Luke, saying something nice?

Devnee walked out of the bathroom and her brother moved out of her way. Didn't block the door, tweak her hair, call her names or anything. In fact, when she turned to look back, he was still staring at her. "Yes?" said Devnee, curving her lips in a teasing sisterly smile.

Luke shook his head. "Dunno," was all he could manage. Then a grin, then a shrug, then once again, "You look great."

She flew up the stairs.

Lying on the little armchair was the outfit she had laid out early last night: jeans, sweatshirt, and sneakers. She could hardly believe it. Had she actually meant to show up in public in that?

I'm feminine now, thought Devnee, and graceful, and beautiful. I will never dress like that again.

She settled on a long black skirt with a filmy brown-and-gold overskirt and, on top, a thin black sweater, very baggy. A gold necklace picked up the glints in the skirt. She debated for some time between gold curlicue earrings and long gold bangles with crystals. When she flicked her hair back so her ears would show, tendrils of dark hair curled against her cheek the way she had always wished her straight plain hair would curl.

Devnee gathered her makeup. She arranged it in a row in front of the lighted mirror and prepared to get to work.

But this Devnee needed no help. She had lashes so dark and lovely that mascara would have been comic. She had cheeks so high and bright that rouge would have been clownish. She had hair so full that a curling iron would be overkill.

She went downstairs for breakfast.

Her parents blinked. "Darling!" said her mother. "You look so lovely!" A funny excitement spread over her mother's face, the same excitement Devnee had felt and corralled: celebration; the ugly duckling is a swan after all; I can relax, my plain baby girl is finally blossoming into a lovely woman.

Her father was just confused. "Did you darken your hair, Dev?"

"Daddy," she said, scolding him gently.

"You don't have to fiddle with what nature gave

you," said her father. "You look beautiful just as you are."

Devnee smiled at him. He smiled back. He said, "You look great, honey. I'm so proud of you these days."

Her mother said, "This year let's get a family portrait done. We've been talking about it for years but we've just never gotten to it. You wear your hair just like that, Dev. You look so lighthearted and happy and" — her mother laughed with surprise — "well, beautiful."

Devnee didn't even want a sip of orange juice; anything might upset the chemical balance that had caused this.

Her father said, "Why don't I drive you to school, sweetheart? I hate for you to put those shoes into the snow."

Devnee smiled graciously at her parents.

The high school lobby was impressive. Sheets of marble, hard and glittering and black, were separated by tiny strips of gold. It looked like a state legislature building, where brilliant — or stupid — decisions were made. Not like a school, where brilliant — or stupid — kids hung out.

Long wide marble steps were topped by large planters, filled with greenery that kids either admired or threw crumpled tissues into, depending on their attitude toward life.

Art exhibits filled the long blank wall.

Students were everywhere. This was the room

in which to meet, to plan, to wave, to talk, and most of all, to be seen.

Devnee entered the lobby.

And she was seen as she had never been seen before.

Girls turned to look at her. Girls whispered to each other about how Devnee wore her hair. Boys tilted their heads the way boys do when they were thinking about what you'd be like.

Devnee stood on display, turning slightly, bestowing on them a side view, and then a slight smile, and finally a slight wave.

Slight, thought Devnee (her insides wildly excited, her outsides calm and perhaps even bored), because I'm used to this, and I hardly think about it anymore.

Nina came running over. Buddy number three. Mean old Nina with her fabulous car and her magnificent sweaters. "Hi, Devnee!" cried Nina. "I love your hair. You look great, Devnee. What a skirt. Where'd you get that? I wanna skirt like that."

Devnee had never had a chance to snub anybody. "I forget," she said, and walked on. Snubbing Nina felt wonderful. She would have to do it often. It was so powerful, so rewarding, to snub somebody.

Devnee's stride, usually halting and unsure, changed. Now she was a dancer, smooth and easy. She could feel how her hair rested on her shoulders, and how her smile decorated her face.

I didn't know you could feel being beautiful

from the inside! she thought. What an extra treat. You don't even have to be in front of a mirror. You can see yourself mirrored in other people.

And I thought the vampire was kidding. I owe him. This is fabulous. This is unbelievable! This is life the way it should be lived!

Everybody commented.

Even the teachers commented.

"I love your hair like that," everybody said to her.

"Gosh, you look great today, Devnee!"

And at lunch, both Trey and William commented. Trey said, "Wow, Dev! Way to go! You look great. Really great."

William nodded, a smile never leaving his face. "This is your year, huh, Devnee? You look great."

Nothing about Devnee Fountain had ever been "great" before. Now it was great to see her, and she looked great, and it was great to be in school.

People kept saying, "What did you do?" as if expecting an answer like "Changed lipstick" or "Used a blow-dryer."

Never in her life had the world come to her.

Never in her life had there been such confidence, such pleasure, in just being alive.

She was not self-conscious. Not worried. Not timid.

She was beautiful.

She ate differently. A beautiful girl did not stuff her face and snatch extras and lean across to grab more, she thought. A beautiful girl spent the entire lunch period nibbling delicately on the rim of a single cracker.

When lunch ended, they all rose, making the usual passes around the cafeteria to dispose of trash, return trays, say hello to people they hadn't spotted before.

Devnee stood very still, accepting homage. Thinking — this is so fabulous. Having people look at you — not because you're new, or you're stupid, or you look funny, or your clothes are weird — but because you are beautiful.

A girl separated herself from the rest and strolled over to Devnee. Devnee knew her. Eleanor. A leader of the senior class. Eleanor was almost regal. She did not seem seventeen, but ageless: like a medieval princess who deserved a stone parapet. "Hello, Devnee," said Eleanor seriously. "I wanted to talk to you about something."

"Of course," said Devnee.

"As you know, the Valentine's Day Dance is coming up," said Eleanor.

Devnee had not known this; in fact, she had not thought of Valentine's Day at all. Now she remembered the holiday: the candy hearts that said BE MINE and KISS ME; the silly cards you addressed to everybody in your class; the red roses your father gave your mother, and the heart-shaped cake she frosted white and sprinkled with coconut.

"Nominations for Valentine Sweetheart must be made this week, and the Sweetheart will be crowned at the dance," said Eleanor.

"How quaint," said Devnee.

Eleanor laughed. "I know. It's rather embarrassing that we still do that kind of thing. But the peasants like it, you know." Eleanor cast a meaningful look at the crowd of the plain and dull that filled most of the cafeteria. She and Devnee laughed together.

Eleanor said, "I'd like to nominate you, Devnee, but of course I want your permission first because so many girls just don't want to be bothered with this beauty queen stuff."

Eleanor, although lovely, was too stern to be nominated for anything as frivolous as Valentine Sweetheart. If Devnee were to name any girl sufficiently frilly, fragile, and lace-edged for such a title, it would be Aryssa.

But I'm Aryssa, thought Devnee.

The pasted-together pieces of her — the old person, the new face, the old memories, the new admiration — they clattered together, and seemed almost to fall apart and hit the ground. Like Cinderella's glass slipper.

She felt broken and afraid.

Where is Aryssa? Is she me? Is she half me? Am I half her? Is she in school today? Does she even exist to come to school? Has her shadow joined the vampire's body? Where is my shadow?

Who is Eleanor nominating — the me who is me, or the Aryssa who is me, or the Aryssa who is not anybody now?

Behind her, William said, "I second the nomination, Devnee."

She turned, trembling, the ice of fear blowing cold between her broken pieces, to see both Trey and William, like a matched pair of horses being readied for a race, steaming and snorting and pawing the ground.

Neither of them wanted Eleanor.

They wanted her.

Devnee stroked the new thick cloud of dark hair on her head as if accepting a different crown. She ducked her head modestly. She smiled her gentlest smile. She said, "That's so sweet of you."

She thought, *Valentine Sweetheart*. The most beautiful girl. The most loved. The most photographed.

I'll need a really special dress. Something in pale pink, something with ribbons.

I'll need a date. Which boy should I take? Trey or William?

She smiled. The joys of being beautiful were like a great basket overflowing with goodies. A nomination here, a handsome boy there, a mirror on this side, a camera soon to go off on that.

They were emerging from the cafeteria into the hallway. The fluorescent lights went strangely dim, and a dark path centered itself on the floor. People shivered slightly in the sudden chilly draft.

The filmy gold-and-black overlay of Devnee's skirt lifted, and swirled, and settled. *He's here.*

*He's in school with me. He's in my mind, even now,
he's reading it, knowing it.*

Eleanor said, "Then you accept the nomination?"

"Of course," said Devnee graciously.

The vampire's laughter, like a maniac with a knife, rose up out of the floor. The rest also heard, and momentarily froze, but then they shrugged, thinking it was nothing, perhaps distant breaking glass.

But it was not nothing.

It was him, and he was here.

A tiny foolish sentence flew back from her memory: a tiny foolish wrong sentence she had allowed herself to think, and now it banged inside her head like metal striking metal, clashed and shouted up inside the thoughts where the vampire could live anytime he chose: I owe him.

She had thought it, and it counted.

I owe him, she had said.

And already he had come to collect the debt.

Chapter 8

Mrs. Cort smiled at the English class. Her smile lingered on Devnee. Even when Victoria said something of great brilliance, Mrs. Cort was hardly distracted. There were only a few minutes left in the period when she said, "Please pass your reports forward. As you know, this counts for one quarter of your grade this marking period."

The usual moans and groans mixed with the shuffling and slapping of papers being passed down the rows.

Devnee's heart missed a beat. She had forgotten to finish her English paper. She had had the rough draft done several days ago, but last night . . . what with everything she had to think about . . . well . . .

"Devnee?" said Mrs. Cort. "I don't seem to have a paper from you."

Devnee opened her new eyes very wide. She bit her lip in the desperate sweet way that worked so well for Aryssa. Of course, Aryssa didn't have Mrs.

Cort. And Mrs. Cort was so solid and sensible. But it was worth a try. Devnee said anxiously, "Oh — I'm so sorry — I — do you think I could pass it in tomorrow? Please?"

"Well . . ." said the teacher.

"I have my rough draft done," said Devnee. "I tried so hard, Mrs. Cort. But my computer crashed and I didn't get it printed out."

"You should have e-mailed me," said William. "I would have printed it for you, Devnee."

"She hasn't really been in town that long," said Victoria. "I mean, it hasn't been easy for Devnee, Mrs. Cort, getting into the rhythm of things."

"It's all right, Devnee," said the teacher understandingly. "These things happen."

The class divided, into those who thought it very fair that a beautiful girl should be allowed an extra day, and those who thought it very cruel that rules were bent for beauty.

They will never bend the rules for Aryssa again, thought Devnee suddenly. Aryssa will have to get her papers in on time and pass her tests and do her lab sheets. Nobody will make excuses for her and nobody will forgive her.

She felt afraid for Aryssa. How would Aryssa stand up to it — she who had always been protected by her looks?

Devnee's heart hardened. Her arteries and veins changed, too, becoming metallic and sterile.

She remembered Aryssa that day. Telling Trey she'd been nice only to get a lab partner to do the scut work for her. Telling Trey the trouble with being nice was that people expected you to go on being nice, even when you were bored to death with it and them. She remembered Trey and Aryssa laughing.

The hardness in her did not quite feel human, it was so steely.

But then, I'm not quite human, she thought. I'm a makeover from a vampire.

The room whirled and spun, as if gravity were letting go of her, as her shadow had let go of her. She would go into some sick horrible orbit occupied by vampires and dark paths, she would —

How silly, she said to herself. Silly, silly dreams. I'm beautiful because I'm growing up at last. Blossoming. New shampoo. Vampires, indeed. What nonsense.

She tossed her hair and felt the beautiful thick curls of it settle on her lovely slim shoulders, felt the eyes of her class turning toward her. She gripped the desk to steady herself, and returned the steady gazes of her classmates. They were surveying her. Admiring. Enjoying. Feasting their eyes on her beauty.

Feasting, thought Devnee, and she gagged.

How did it happen? What did he do, exactly? Is Aryssa all right?

How much red there suddenly seemed to be in the room. Red fingernails, red jewelry, red skirts, and somewhere, red blood.

I want to be beautiful, but I don't want —

Well, it probably wasn't *really* like that. He probably didn't *really* —

English ended.

Her silly twisted daydream and dark fantasies ended.

Victoria and William smiled at her. She basked in it. She had never had a day in which the world came to her rescue and smiled back. Never a day in which there was such pleasure just to be alive.

She stood up gracefully, smoothing her pretty skirt, readying herself to join them.

Victoria and William leaned against each other, laughed together, wrapped arms around each other, and headed in tandem for their next class. She had not seen them as a pair, was certainly not expecting the jolt of jealousy that ran through her.

She gritted her teeth but stopped that immediately, knowing it could not be a beautiful expression. She whirled to find Trey. Trey would be alone now that there was no Aryssa here.

But Trey had caught up to Victoria and William. He bounced alongside them, a jock puppy tagging along.

Devnee never forced herself on people, but she knew her beauty did no good unless people were looking at it. She rushed after them, speeding past, and then slowing herself, lingering like the end of a dance. And sure enough, their haste ended, the twosome softened, self-interest dwindled. They feasted their eyes on Devnee.

"What's everybody doing after school?" said William.

"Guess I'd better check on Aryssa," said Trey, running up the wall to leave his shoe prints.

"Is she sick, do you think?" said Victoria worriedly.

Trey admired his shoe prints. "Nah. She had an English paper, too, you know. She's always sick the day a paper is due." Trey laughed. William and Victoria laughed.

They still think Aryssa is beautiful, thought Devnee, so they still forgive her for being dumb. What will happen when Trey goes over there?

She imagined Trey, staring in confusion, perhaps in horror, at the thing Aryssa would be now. She imagined him reaching out to touch her, heal her, and then shrinking back because of the change in her. She imagined him seeing something on her throat, frowning, leaning forward, saying, *Aryssa, what happened to you?*

And Aryssa.

Would she know what had happened? Would she say, *A vampire came in the night. Devnee sent him. Remember the creepy girl who used to live in the mansion? Well, another creepy one lives there now. Devnee chose me, Devnee picked me out and ruined me and took all I had, Trey!*

And Trey. What would he do next? Would he run away from her? Would he turn on Devnee? Would he tell the rest of the world? Would he shout: *Do you know how she got that beauty? Do you know the trade she made?*

Devnee faltered, touching the wall for support.

Terror infected her lungs like a parasite.

It can't be real. There is no vampire. There is no such thing as a vampire. I don't believe in vampires. Nothing happened to Aryssa; she just didn't get her paper written.

Time had changed character for Devnee. It had the capacity to absorb her, like the center of a cyclone. While she had been in the cyclone, evil thoughts whirling, William and Victoria had moved on, and Trey left for his car. She was alone in the hall with Nina. Nasty Nina with nothing but money and sweaters. *I must not fall into my thoughts like that again,* Devnee told herself. *I must keep my thoughts on beauty and on myself.*

Nina and Devnee had to turn a corner, enter a stairwell, head down another wing. When they passed a girls' room, Devnee ducked inside. She had to check the mirror. See if she was still beautiful.

Yes.

The beauty had not gone anywhere.

Nina said, "You're exactly like Aryssa, you know."

Devnee flinched.

"Always going to the girls' room to look in a mirror. Isn't it enough to be beautiful, Devnee? Do you have to have proof ten times a day? What do girls like you see in that mirror? Why don't you feel safe? It's going to last, you know. Either you're beautiful or you aren't."

Devnee laughed nervously.

She went to the frosted glass window of the girls' room and tilted it inward and open for fresh air.

It was snowing lightly. New-fallen snow blanketed the old ugly crust blackened by car exhaust.

Like me, thought Devnee Fountain. I, too, am new-fallen.

I sold Aryssa.

Was it worth it?

The very second she questioned whether the beauty was worth it, her beauty began to slide off. Like a mud mask. It peeled away from her skin and slid toward the window.

No! she thought, putting her hands up to hold her cheeks, hold on to her beauty. You gave it to me, you can't take it back!

If it isn't worth it to you, I'll give it to somebody else, the vampire said from right inside her mind. She had forgotten that he shared it with her now. That he could live there if he chose.

If I'm not real, said the vampire, *you aren't beautiful anyway, are you?*

She turned frantically toward the window, where outside the world lay dim and wintry.

You've insulted me, said the vampire. *Insulted my gift.*

She could see his dark path well — a shadow cast where there was nothing to cast it.

It's real, you're real! she said to the dark path. *I take it back, it was all real!*

Her face was half on, half off. She could not turn back to Nina or look around toward the row of mirrors above the sinks.

You are a vampire, she said to him. *You are real.*

Inside her head the vampire raised his eyebrows.

Her beauty trembled, unsure, not quite leaving, not quite staying.

And I really gave you Aryssa, she admitted. *And it was worth it.*

Her beauty returned. It returned with a permanency that was solid and sure. It would never slide off again. She had Aryssa's beauty and the vampire had Aryssa.

And it was worth it, she said to herself firmly.

Chapter 9

Devnee walked slowly to her locker and then slowly to the lobby.

People smiled at her. They continued to remark on how nice she looked today — was it her birthday or something?

Devnee had never been the center of anything. Even at her own birthday parties, it always felt as if the little girls she had invited were being polite.

Today she was the center of it all.

She had not known that beauty was literally pivotal: that heads would turn, bodies would turn, eyes would turn — all to look at Devnee Fountain.

She had not known how differently she would stand and pose; how her chin would lift, and her head would tilt, and her eyes would tease.

Usually she could leave school — any school, the last one, this one — in a few seconds.

Today, what with talking and waving and smiling and flirting, it took a long time. There was so much to do, so much to say.

This is how perfect people live, thought Devnee, stunned.

They're busy. Busy being beautiful.

She laughed with the sheer joy of it and, listening to the sound of her laugh, realized that it, too, was different; not just an ordinary everyday garden-variety laugh — it was a beautiful cascade of joy. Everybody laughed with her, and the afternoon was free and soft and lovely.

And the real Devnee — her soul, her personality — was at last where it belonged: in a perfect, matching body.

She knew now why they had bought the house with the tower. It was because she, Devnee, was destined for beauty. The vampire had simply straightened out an error of birth. It was only right and just.

Finally the crush of students in the lobby dwindled, as people went on to sports events, or orthodontist appointments, or the pizza place.

And Trey came back to school.

She saw his car coming to the front drive. Such an ordinary car for such a fabulous boy. A dull four-door sedan. Matronly. Middle-aged. And yet it didn't matter, because with Trey on the inside it was incredibly exciting and wonderful.

He parked right in front of the front door.

Not allowed.

Students had a student parking lot. Even disabled students had to park down below and come in the bottom entry.

She wondered if handsome boys, like beautiful girls, could get away with things. Was Trey parking there because he knew nobody would tow his car?

Trey came up the stairs, opened the lobby door, and looked around.

He looked wrong.

He looked off balance.

He looked — well — spooked.

"Trey?" said Devnee.

He seemed to see her with difficulty. As if focusing his eyes were hard. As if she were coming and going from his sight. He walked over unsteadily and said, "Devnee. I'm so glad somebody's still here. I just went to see Aryssa. She's — she's —"

He couldn't finish.

Devnee's hair prickled. Her skin stood out from her bones. Her soul stiffened. She said, "She's what, Trey?"

He shook his head. "I don't know how to describe it." Trey shuddered.

Devnee said softly, "Let's go to the Doughnut House and talk about it."

"How did you know I love the Doughnut House?" said Trey, half laughing and half still upset.

How *did* I know? thought Devnee, and now half of Devnee, too, was upset. She could feel the vampire tickling the edges of her mind and she hated it — that he could live there like that, that he was part of her and she was part of him.

In Trey's car they went to the Doughnut House. They could not find a space right in front and parked down a block. They had to walk slowly, picking their way around slush and ice piles.

A guy in a mason's dump truck honked at Devnee and grinned.

A city bus driver tapped his horn and gave her a thumbs-up.

Two men on a rooftop repairing shingles whistled.

A woman in a store window changing the display gazed at her with the complex admiration of a plain woman for a beautiful one.

Once inside, snuggled up to the counter and each other, they ordered hot chocolate, which she loved to stir more than to drink. Although she loved jelly doughnuts, they were messy, and beautiful girls did not risk eating messy foods, so she had a plain sugar doughnut instead.

"See, she's all kind of — well — lumpy," said Trey. He ate his first jelly doughnut in precisely two bites. Two huge raspberry-running bites. The raspberry filling dotted the corners of his mouth like blood.

Devnee swallowed, although she had nothing in her mouth but panic.

"Aryssa is always dumb," said Trey. "I mean, that goes with the territory." He half laughed, half shrugged. "But this time — I don't know what's wrong with her. She's kind of heavy and thick and — well" — Trey looked as if he could not figure the next word out — "ugly," he said at last. "She's really ugly, Devnee."

Ugly? thought Devnee. She looks like I used to? I wasn't ugly! I was just ordinary. Wasn't I?

Trey said, "I mean, I didn't want to spend time with her. The kind of girl that guys puke if they get stuck with. You know. A real dog."

Devnee was chilled. Trey could not have been with Aryssa ten minutes. Did he really judge completely, entirely on looks?

Devnee could not help herself. She said, "Maybe Aryssa is just coming down with something. You know. A bug. A virus. Maybe in a few days she'll feel better and all that."

Trey shook his head. "Nah. I could tell. This is for good."

"Was there" — Devnee paused, feeling her way — "anything else different?"

"Like what?" said Trey, eating a second doughnut. Another two bites and it vanished. She wondered if the vampire's appetite was that great. If the vampire had —

For a terrible cruel moment, it seemed to her that Trey was also a vampire. She gripped the hard edges of the yellow counter in both hands, until the rims dented her palms, and then she looked back at Trey. No, he was still handsome, sexy, impressive.

He said, "So, Dev." He grinned, putting Aryssa on the discard pile with his raspberry-stained napkins. "There's a dance coming up."

Her heart pounded. No boy had ever even hinted that he might like to take Devnee Fountain to a dance.

"A Valentine's dance," said Trey.

They smiled at each other; small knowing smiles.

He said, "I hear Eleanor nominated you for Sweetheart."

She ducked her head modestly.

"Come on," said Trey. "You know how gorgeous you are."

She laughed.

He said, "It's funny. I misjudged you. I guess with new kids, it's kind of easy. They're nervous and you get thrown off and don't really realize who they are. I mean — I was thinking you were —" Trey shrugged again. It was a frequent habit with him. It was, Devnee suddenly thought, almost girlish. He used his broad shoulders to escape the ends of sentences the way Aryssa had used her beauty.

He said, "So."

She raised her eyebrows.

They both laughed.

"Want to come with me to the Valentine's dance?" said Trey. He knew she would. They both knew she would. Beautiful people, she realized, always understood what other beautiful people were thinking.

She was in no rush to answer.

It had also come to her that beautiful people were not desperate.

They were not threatened. They were in no hurry. They could say yes if they felt like it . . . or no.

She said to Trey, "I think that would be lovely, Trey."

"Like you," he said, and he preened, and this time it did not seem girlish, but more like a peacock flaring its feathers, and it came to Devnee that there was nothing to Trey but his exterior.

He was a boy who could dump a girl in, literally, a heartbeat.

All because that girl had a bad day.

Inside her head, the vampire corrected her. Bad night, actually, said the vampire, and the vampire laughed and laughed and laughed, and the laugh came out of Devnee's mouth, and Trey was startled at the length of her laughter, but he joined in, because life amused him, and beauty amused him, and as long as Devnee remained beautiful, he would remain with Devnee.

Chapter 10

Luke's basketball game began at 6:15. They all had to go and cheer him on.

She was furious at this waste of time until she arrived.

People actually turned to look at her, flinging hoods off their heads, tucking scarves down, adjusting glasses. "Who's that?" they whispered to each other.

"New girl," came the answer. "Lives in the mansion at the bottom of the hill."

"She's beautiful!"

It worked everywhere, this beauty, with everyone. With adults and teenagers, with teachers and toddlers.

A crowd of kids from the high school decorated the top two bleachers on the right. In her old school Devnee would not even have tried to join the crowd. She would have known she was unwanted and a pest. In this new school Devnee would not have tried to join. She knew how people like Aryssa and

Trey saw her: as the kind of girl who never understood that you didn't really want her there.

But this was now, this was beauty; she climbed easily up the bleachers and people who saw her coming smiled and moved apart, knowing that she of course was going to the top.

She hardly even knew the kids at the top, but she joined them without a flicker of concern, and sure enough, they were delighted to have her. Devnee basked in their attention, and went with them at halftime to buy candy from the fund-raiser in the lobby, and when her brother made baskets everybody in her row cheered extra hard. Not because she was related to Luke — but because Luke was related to her.

She was the one who mattered now.

There was only one bad moment.

She was introduced to Aryssa's parents.

"Where is Aryssa?" said everybody else.

"She doesn't feel well," said her parents uncertainly. "She's under the weather." They looked at each other, deeply upset, confused, disoriented. Perhaps they did not even know the teenage girl who had gotten up that morning.

They were nice people.

They reminded Devnee of her own parents. Solid, dull, uninteresting, ordinary people. How did they have a daughter like Aryssa? she wondered.

But they don't now.

Aryssa isn't, now.

How hot the gym was. How loudly the sneakers squealed, how cruelly the cameras flashed.

"Do you feel faint, Devnee?" said one of the girls solicitously. "Want me to help you? Somebody buy Devnee a soda."

Two boys bounced down the bleachers to buy Devnee a soda.

At last, at last, she was alone in the tower. Her family had wasted so much of her time, fawning over her, complimenting her. Suffocating her. Really, couldn't they tell she had better things to do than fuss with them?

She was strangely angry at them. Why did they have such a light in their eyes? Where had that light been for the first fifteen years? Why did it have to take beauty to make them proud of her?

What if they find out? she thought. What if they learned what I did to get this beauty?

There were questions to ask. Futures to decide. Facts to learn.

She did not bother turning on the light.

He was more likely to come in the dark anyhow. She waited.

He came by mouth, teeth first, like green shoots in the spring, moss covered. He wiped them on his black cloak and the fungus was gone, leaving stains on the cloak, leaving his teeth white and gleaming and ready.

Her blood seemed to cease circulating, as if it

knew what those fangs were for, what those teeth had been doing, what could happen next.

All the things she had meant to say evaporated. Her head was as empty as her soul.

Devnee sat absolutely still in her bed, watching the smile drip, and advance. To her surprise, her shadow joined her. In the dark her shadow was soft and fuzzy, like a friend. Like somebody on her team.

The vampire smiled, and something phosphorescent oozed from his fangs. His mouth was a cave, and stalactites were forming even as she watched.

She knew better than to let her terror show. She said to her shadow, "You stay here! You hear me?"

The shadow said nothing.

The vampire said, "A nice girl, Devnee . . ."

But I'm not nice, she thought. Trey isn't, either. He goes only by looks. But that's what I go by of course, and I'm not nice, either; we have proof of that now, don't we?

"Say what you have to say," said Devnee sharply, "and get out. I have to get some sleep."

"Beauty sleep," said the vampire, "isn't that what they call it?"

She closed her eyes, although it was difficult in his presence. She felt as if she needed several more sets of eyes, so some would always be open, always be a sentry to protect her in the night.

"Yes," breathed the vampire, "beauty sleep. A

different kind of sleep than you have ever had before, isn't it, Devnee? A sleep in which you are beautiful! What a wonderful feeling. To be beautiful at last."

His voice was soft and rumbly as a purring cat's.

Her shadow lay back on the bed with her. She felt sleep coming, and he was right — it was different.

"You are glad you made that wish, aren't you?" he whispered.

She nodded against the pillow. She was glad. How could she not be glad? Some things have a price, she thought. I just have to accept that. Aryssa has to accept that. I accepted being plain for fifteen years, now it's her turn, so there.

"Of course, a nice girl would give it back," said the vampire briskly.

Give it back?

She opened her eyes.

"I mean, is this really kind to Aryssa?" said the vampire.

Of course it wasn't kind. It was horrible.

But —

A hundred *buts* came into her head. But I like being beautiful. But it isn't my fault. But I didn't go out and get this beauty. You're the bad guy! "You gave it to me," she said finally. "It's up to you what happens to it."

The vampire laughed. "No, my dear. It's up to *you*. Isn't that a wonderful thought? Aren't you thrilled? You have the power to go back to being plain again. You have the power to decide to be dull and boring. Just wallpaper. Just another sample in the book. Just another faceless member of the crowd." He had retracted his teeth like turtle legs; his smile was sweet and kind. "You can make Aryssa happy and beautiful again, Devnee. What a wonderful feeling! You can be kind."

She was holding hands with her shadow.

Or was it an extension of the vampire's cloak? Both were thick and cloudy and velvety. But this had a taste. It tasted of vapor and mold. She gagged slightly. She tried to remember why she had actually wanted the vampire to come tonight. She had had questions. What were they?

"Of course," said the vampire, "everyone has a streak of selfishness in her. Some of us more than others. But it's inevitably present in a human being. It's simply a matter of tapping the selfishness." He studied his horrid fingernails in a girlish way, as if his wrinkled foil needed a touch-up.

She envisioned him in some world alien to her own, in front of some evil mirror, inspecting himself, admiring himself.

The vampire raised his eyebrows. "But my dear, that's exactly what you do. I saw you today, in front of the mirror, inspecting and admiring."

"You followed me?" She was outraged.

"I *am* you."

"Don't be disgusting!" she shouted.

The vampire smiled and this time held his

hand neatly over his mouth, keeping his weapons delicately hidden.

She said in a low voice, "Aryssa isn't actually hurt, is she?"

"Of course not, my dear. How could you think that of me? It doesn't hurt. Aryssa is simply . . . rather . . . tuckered out."

Devnee was feeling rather tuckered out herself. But she doubted if it was the same thing.

The vampire said, "Sleep well, my dear."

Right, she thought.

"Tomorrow in school . . ." He laughed gaily, like a child going to a picnic. "You will cross paths with Aryssa. My path will be there, too, of course. Just another shadow, you will think. But of course there is nothing ordinary about my path." The vampire smiled proudly at his dark path.

He said, "It will happen in the lobby, my dear. Such a pretty room. All that glittering marble in which you — the beautiful stunning you — will be reflected. And as the paths intersect . . . yours, Aryssa's, mine . . . you will have the choice, dear girl, of whether to stay beautiful . . . or . . . be kind."

He blinked several times, as if slamming doors with his eyes.

He slid away toward the shutters and she felt her shadow being suctioned off her, and she clung to the shadow, holding it in her fingers, and this contest she won; the shadow was hers.

But the choice was still to come.

She could be nice. Or she could be beautiful.

* * *

"Oh, what a beautiful morning!"

It was an old, old song. Devnee did not know where it came from.

Her mother was singing in the kitchen. "Oh, what a beautiful morning!" She could hear the shuffling slide of dancing feet. For her mother, the day, her life, her daughter — it was all so beautiful it had to be sung about and danced to.

Sun was everywhere.

Snow had fallen during the night, and the sun glittered on the pristine white world, and gleamed through every window and sparkled on every surface.

Devnee went downstairs to find her family in wonderful moods, her mother trilling, her father bouncing, her brother leaping.

Her mother kissed her on each cheek. "Isn't this a beautiful day?" she cried.

Her father hugged her. "I *do* have a beautiful daughter," he said proudly, holding her off for a better view and then hugging her again.

Even her brother grinned and saluted.

Always before she had seen *them* as worthless and *herself* as worthy. But was this true? She who worked with vampires? Just who was worth anything around here?

"Last night at the game?" said Luke to his sister. "Yeah?"

"One of my friends wanted to know who you were," Luke said. He was pleased. He was proud.

Luke — who used to be sickened that he had a blood relationship with Devnee.

Blood. I must not think of blood.

Her father spread strawberry jam on a toasted bagel and for a minute seemed to be sticking his knife into a jar of congealed blood.

Devnee held on to herself, and for one queer horrifying moment her self seemed to detach as the shadow had, leaving her with nothing but the beautiful shell.

"Which friend?" she asked Luke. She picked up her orange juice. It was crimson. She nearly spilled it.

"Cranberry juice," said her mother, chirping like a canary. "I thought it would make such a pretty change."

They sat together, eating hastily. Mornings were never leisurely. Too many people rushing too many places. And yet she had time to look at her family, and see them anew.

"Jesse," said her brother. "Too young for you. But among your admirers, Dev."

No sarcasm.

Their father said, "I've been thinking about that family portrait. I do want to do it. I've got such a nice family, and we're at such a nice stage in our lives. We've fit into this town so well. We all love our jobs and school and house. Don't we?"

"A beautiful family," agreed her mother.

Devnee's hair prickled. Her mother was much prettier than usual. Her mother was glowing and —

No.

No, the vampire had not also corrupted her mother.

No, these things could not be. It was Devnee who lived in the tower, and Devnee who had made the bargain. Her mother was innocent. Had to be. That's what mothers were.

Devnee thought of the test to come. The meeting in the lobby. The crossing of the paths of Aryssa, Devnee, and the vampire.

I can be kind or I can be beautiful. I cannot be both. That's so unfair! He has no right to put me in that kind of situation.

This is all his fault, for being hungry and greedy.

None of this is my fault.

Devnee gathered her school things, put on her coat, remembered her scarf and mittens, but did not put them on; carried them as colorful accessories instead. They went out the door, Devnee to her bus and Luke to his.

Luke ran on ahead, because Luke ran everywhere, pumping muscles wherever he could, getting his daily pleasure from the mere throbbing of his own legs.

She walked sedately after him, aware of her beauty; aware that she, too, sparkled like snow.

Her shadow kept its distance.

It came . . . but it was not attached.

It was judging her. Waiting to see what happened in the lobby.

Chapter 11

In the lobby Eleanor, queenly and elegant, flourished a decorated cardboard box in which Sweetheart nominations had been dropped. It was a shoebox, the kind that in grade school you decorated with red construction paper and lace doilies and cutouts from women's magazines, and cut a slit in the top of. Then on Valentine's Day you collected those silly little cards from everybody in class.

In grade school, the teachers made everybody be nice.

If you weren't going to give a card to everybody, you couldn't give cards at all.

And yet you could still tell who was loved and who was not.

Perhaps the cards for the popular girls were larger. Or lacier.

Perhaps the party given on Saturday included only a few.

Perhaps the cupcake handed to you by the

number one kid in the class had less icing on it than the one he gave to his real friend.

But in elementary school, on Valentine's Day, you had to be nice.

"Hi, Devnee," said Eleanor. "How are you today?"

"Fine, thanks, how are you?"

"Couldn't be better. You look lovely. You must tell me how to put on makeup like that."

Devnee was wearing none.

Eleanor opened the cardboard vote box, which was surely not proper democratic procedure, but then, as Eleanor pointed out, what is democratic about a princess?

A pile of paper squares lay on the bottom of the box.

Her name was written again and again: DEVNEE FOUNTAIN, DEVNEE FOUNTAIN, DEVNEE FOUNTAIN FOR VALENTINE SWEETHEART.

"Of course, these are only nominations," said Eleanor. "We don't know till the Sweetheart Dance who has actually been voted Sweetheart." She laughed a knowing, superior laugh. "I'm not worried, though. Are you, Devnee?"

Devnee laughed, also, equally knowing, equally superior.

A boy she did not know smiled nicely at her. "Guess you're going to be the Sweetheart, huh?"

She gave him her flirtiest smile. "Are you voting for me?"

He blushed. He shuffled a little, embarrassed

by attention from somebody as important and special as Devnee. "Well, actually . . . I guess I'm voting for my own girl," he said. And put his arm around a plain and ordinary girl at his side, and smiled at her. Smiled with love.

Devnee's heart hurt.

For one incredible moment she actually yearned to be his girl — to get his vote no matter who was prettier.

But she set that thought aside.

William came into the lobby. What a hunk he was!

She waited for William to come to her and say something sweet.

But his eyes were elsewhere. His eyes were on Victoria. Devnee was amazed. Impressive as Victoria was, interesting, intriguing, smart, all that — still, William could do so much better. William could have Devnee.

But William's eyes lingered on Victoria, and eventually he grew courageous and let his hand linger on her, too. Just barely. Just the back of her waist. But Victoria seemed oblivious to William's intentions. That was an act of course; nobody on earth could be oblivious to William.

Aryssa walked in.

Perhaps it was an exaggeration to say "walked."

She slumped in, dragging her feet. She moved as if she were a dead weight on the end of a tow rope.

Hardly anybody looked at her.

Only Victoria seemed to recognize Aryssa. "Aryssa," said Victoria, going over instantly, not even noticing as William's hand fell from her waist, leaving him behind without a thought. "Aryssa, what's wrong? You really look down and out!"

Aryssa's smile did not quite appear. It was just a feeble slow lip twitch. "I think I — I think I'm tired," she said.

"You should have stayed home another day," said Victoria. "You don't look well enough to be in school."

"It's the last day for nominations for Sweetheart," said Aryssa. "I wanted to be here."

Several people looked at her with disgusted laughter and pity. They whispered softly to each other. Devnee knew what they were saying — that lump? A dance queen? Please.

Eleanor said softly to Devnee, "Aryssa's let herself go so badly. I don't know how she could possibly be anybody's Sweetheart. She looks more like anybody's candy wrapper. Ready for the trash."

Eleanor's group laughed meanly.

Be kind to her, thought Devnee, a little shocked.

A dark path oozed out from a crack in the marble. The crack was filled with a strip of gold, and the purity of the gold remained intact, even though the dark path tried to compromise it.

I could be gold, thought Devnee. I could give up my beauty. Right now. Aryssa could go back to who she is, and people would still admire her, and she would have Trey.

And I would be kind.

And plain.

Dull.

Unloved.

The dark path unrolled, like a stained and moth-eaten carpet.

She stared at it, wondering where it was going, where it would stop, who would trip on it and fall in.

"Hi, Devnee," said another boy. "Going to be Sweetheart soon, huh?"

She smiled back as sweetly as she knew how, to show that her heart was a match for her beauty.

William caught up to Victoria and said, "Aryssa, you want me to drive you back home? You really look wiped out."

Victoria gave him a look.

William did not know how to interpret it and looked nervously back.

Victoria said to Aryssa, "William and I are nominating you for Sweetheart, Aryssa." She gave Aryssa a hug.

Devnee thought of the last person to give Aryssa a hug and quivered.

Person? said the vampire in her head. *Really, my dear. I am not a person.*

Get out of my mind! said Devnee silently.

Why? I like it in here. It's so similar to my own.

Devnee flinched, and Eleanor, next to her, said in that snippy successful voice, "Problem?"

"Of course not," said Devnee, laughing.

Kindness brightened the receiver. Aryssa was

recovering slightly because Victoria was being nice. Because William was there. She didn't look beautiful again, of course, but at least she didn't look like a dead body.

Devnee was relieved. She didn't have to do anything after all. Aryssa was going to be fine. Devnee did not have to get involved or sacrifice anything. Victoria would take care of it.

She had answered Eleanor correctly. There was no problem.

The dark path rolled on.

The shadow of Aryssa, the shadow of Devnee, and the shadow of the vampire intersected on the gleaming marble, and for one moment they could not be distinguished. They had, as shadows do, blended.

Interesting, said the vampire in her head.

Go away, said Devnee.

I actually thought you would be kind, said the vampire. *You come from a kind family. I attempted to enter your mother's mind, you know. She could not quite communicate with me. That happens with nice people. Honor required that I give her daughter a second chance.*

Go away! screamed Devnee.

He did not answer. His dark path stayed in the lobby.

I didn't have to be kind, Devnee told him. Victoria was kind for me.

He laughed.

They could almost hear it, the students in the

lobby, and they looked around vaguely, as if wondering whose CD player that was.

Nobody can be kind for you, my dear, said the vampire. *But I don't mind, of course. I have you now. There's no escape, my dear. You and I, Devnee Fountain, are a team.*

"Now you go home, drink a gallon of orange juice, take tons of vitamins, and sleep all weekend." Victoria beamed at Aryssa. William got out his car keys. "Then you'll be fine."

She won't be fine, thought Devnee. I stole her fineness. You can nominate her for all the Valentine's Day Dances in the world and she still won't be fine. Because I decided against it. I chose beauty over kindness.

Trey entered the lobby from the opposite end. He did not see Aryssa, or Victoria, or William. How could he? The glitter and glitz of Devnee took up all his attention. He galloped across the room toward her.

He was tough, and half violent, stunning without being handsome.

And I was right, thought Devnee, getting ready for Trey.

Beauty over kindness any day.

But "any day" no longer existed for Devnee Fountain.

The old Devnee — her days had been any old

day, one blending seamlessly into another, dull, fogged, pointless days.

Now the days spun and sparkled.

The exciting crowd burbled around her, and she within it. Aryssa did not come back for a week, and when she did, even Victoria and William seemed only to half know her. Aryssa was a half person.

Devnee was relieved.

Now she need only half worry.

Aryssa probably couldn't even tell what had happened. Aryssa was just a thing now. A half event. To whom people gave half their attention.

Or none.

Chapter 12

A Valentine's Day Dance.

Thanks to a generous parent in the restaurant business, it was not held in any gym or cafeteria, but at the Silver Cloud. This sounded to Devnee like a Montana ranch or an America's Cup sailing ship.

It was a perfectly named restaurant. Silver walls — yes, silver! They reflected a thousand times more than the dark marble of the school lobby. Crystal prisms hung from a thousand ceiling lamps, and tiny hidden lights, like miniature Christmas tree lights, rimmed unexpected ledges. Rainbows flitted from one crystal to another, and colored shadows danced on the silver walls.

The high ceilings were hidden by something gauzy that Devnee could not quite see; truly cloud-like.

She felt airborne. Felt ethereal. Felt beautiful.

She floated, because silver clouds floated.

Trey was a wonderful dancer, and the dance was a wonderful dance.

And Devnee Fountain had no competition in the beauty department. She had never been worshiped. She had never even been noticed. And at this dance, she reigned.

Something had changed inside her as well.

She could feel things happening in the room, happening in other people, that she had never felt before.

She knew, absolutely knew, that every girl in the room wished she could look like Devnee Fountain. She could *feel* their wishes. The room was full of wishes. Quivery, like gelatin, the wishes cluttered the room, and she felt as if she were swimming among them.

Wishes for beauty, for grace, for love, for boys, for more, and more, and more, and more.

She was glad they were so far away from the tower, and the shutters, and the hemlocks of the vampire.

Too many wishes here for him.

A hundred girls in a hundred pretty dresses swirled by, and their wishes throbbed in her ears and pulsed against her heart.

How easily his fangs . . .

"Why are you doing that?" said Trey.

"What?"

"Putting your hand over your mouth like that."

She had not been aware of doing that.

"Every time you laugh, you cover your mouth," said Trey. "I mean, what for? Something wrong with your teeth?"

Her laugh was tinged with fear. Did her hand know, as the shadow had known, that Devnee was no longer right? Was the hand trying to cover her up, as the shadow was trying to escape? If she looked in a mirror right now, along with the beauty, would she see long, pointed, dripping —

She laughed. She said, "Silly habit. Now I'll break it." She kissed Trey on the cheek.

Trey kissed her back. On the lips. "Keep breaking it," he said.

They were doing this when William and Victoria waltzed up. They didn't really waltz, of course; Devnee had never actually seen anybody waltz. But they were so graceful together the only possible dance word was *waltz*.

Victoria said, "I was just wondering, Trey. Not to be rude or anything." She smiled gently at both of them, and then especially at Devnee. "But I phoned Aryssa and couldn't get much out of her. What exactly is wrong? Why isn't she coming back to school?"

Trey frowned a confused little-boy frown, as one bewildered by global events beyond control. "I dunno," he said. Very little boy. Carefully not associating himself with a former girlfriend gone weird.

"Well," said Victoria, "her spirits are so low these days that the rest of us have done a lot of thinking, and we think that in order to make her feel better, maybe coax her back, get her laughing again, all that —"

What was coming here? Devnee felt terribly threatened. She tried to keep a sweet kindly smile on her face, but she was trembling all over. What had Victoria done?

"— we should elect her Sweetheart even though she's not at the dance," said Victoria. "I've got enough votes, I think." Victoria repeated her kindly smile, and Devnee wanted to swat it.

Where did Victoria come off, snatching the Sweetheart crown away from Devnee minutes before she won it? *I am the most beautiful here!* thought Devnee. *And those are the rules.*

"That's a great idea," said Trey, who clearly could not care less.

"Isn't it?" said William, who clearly cared a lot. "Victoria thought of it herself." He stared adoringly at Victoria. Then he turned to Devnee. "Do we have your vote, too, Dev?"

The blackmail of it.

What could she say, here in the middle of the room, with admirers listening? *No, you can't have my vote! I want me!*

"Of course," said Devnee warmly. "That's a lovely, lovely idea, Victoria. I can't believe I didn't think of it myself."

Victoria gave Devnee a thorough look. Victoria definitely knew that Devnee would never have thought of it, and if it had been suggested, would have vetoed it with all her power.

And so Aryssa was elected Sweetheart. It was unanimous.

And the night, which had been Devnee's, became Victoria's.

Victoria had not even been nominated, and yet she became the dance's real sweetheart. Because she had one: a truly sweet heart.

Devnee had to stop using the electric blanket because the wiring in the house was so old and faulty it kept failing, and she'd wake up freezing under this paper-thin nothing. Now she had two wool blankets and a thick puff of a comforter. Devnee wrapped up mummy-style.

"Really," said the vampire mildly, "this is not necessary."

Devnee simply looked at him. "It's necessary," she said.

His cape fluttered around him like pond scum.

"Get out of my room," said Devnee. "I want to be alone."

He was amused. "You are never alone now, my dear."

It was true. She had not been alone in many, many days. He had infected her, and she carried him like a virus in her soul. I wish he would disappear, she thought. Just leave my beauty and disappear. I wish I were as smart as Victoria. I'd think of a way to outwit him.

The vampire's laugh rattled like hard candy falling on a bare floor. "You have a most interesting mind, my dear. Filled with wishes. You are never satisfied. I like that in a girl. Opens many doors."

"Get out of my mind!" said Devnee.

The vampire shook his head. His neck did not rotate as human necks did, so that when he shook the head the entire trunk of his body shook with it, giving him a sickening Jell-O effect.

"You let me in," said the vampire. "You didn't have to, you know. You had a choice. You could have been satisfied with what you were."

"I'm satisfied now," said Devnee sharply. "So leave me alone."

"Are you really satisfied?" said the vampire. "Odd. That's not the wish path I see emanating from your heart. I see you wanting William now. Because you know the real Trey, and the real Trey is something of a disappointment. The skin-deep variety always is. And William really loves Victoria, whereas Trey loves only a beautiful escort. Victoria, you know, is brilliant. William is one of those rare young men attracted to brains." The vampire smiled and it lit his eyes, incandescent lights inside his skull.

"Aryssa's going to be all right now," said Devnee. "The dance voted her Sweetheart to make her feel better."

The vampire glowed. "It worked wonderfully, too, my dear. She felt much better." He studied his fingernails. The flesh on his long thin fingers was pink. Not the darkened patches of fruit going bad.

Not spongy as if swollen with rot beneath the skin. But nice, healthy —

"I have just had another excellent meal," said the vampire.

Devnee's heart almost stopped. "Another one?"

"Once the path is open, it's open," he said. "Naturally I will use all of Aryssa that is available." He giggled like a little kid who had just TP'd the teacher's car. Not a vampire. He said, "Of course, there isn't much left of Aryssa. Still . . ."

Oh, Aryssa! Devnee was sick with the knowing of it. That he had gone back!

Those fangs — did they?

That cape — did it?

That laugh — that smell — those glittering evil eyes?

"Now, now, we can't hide from what we've done," said the vampire. "In part, we cannot hide because . . ."

She forced herself to look at him.

". . . because . . . we're going to do it again."

"What are you talking about? I wanted to be beautiful and I am!"

"I thought you wanted it all," said the vampire. His speech was slippery as silk and cruel as boredom.

All.

Oh, yes.

Oh, how she wanted it all.

She wanted riches, too. And brains. And fame. And talent.

She was weak with all the things she wanted; they turned her knees to jelly and made her heart pound.

She studied her own fingernails, so long and lovely and polished and perfect. I'm beautiful now, she said to herself; that's enough.

"Enough?" said the vampire. "Is it really enough, my dear?"

She caught her breath.

He said, "Envision, if you will, English class. Envision yourself, if you will, as the sort of person who simply gets A's, without effort or design."

There were people like that. Victoria was one.

When asked "Did you study?" Victoria would laughingly reply, "I never study." It was true. Devnee would sit consumed with envy. Even if she studied for a month, she could not get the grade Victoria got without effort.

"Ah, yes," said the vampire, "just so."

She threw a pillow at him but he was not there by the time it passed through the air. In fact, when she turned to look, she could not quite find him. She could sense his darkness and smell his mold, but he was as out of focus as a bad photograph.

Did Aryssa smell that? she thought. When he — when it — when —

She said, "I'm beautiful. That's enough. Go away."

"Enough," whispered the vampire. "Enough. I doubt it, Devnee, my dear."

She was very still.

"Perhaps . . ." said the vampire, his voice as

level as a lily pad on still water. "Perhaps . . . you could have Victoria's brains."

Victoria, who was nice. Victoria, who was generous. Victoria, who was thoughtful. Victoria, who was loved by William.

She would like to have Victoria's brains . . . but the vampire would then have Victoria. And would go to her again and again, as he was going to Aryssa. Victoria would be over.

No, I won't take Victoria's brains.

But wouldn't it be glorious to be brilliant? And witty? And have people stop talking and lean forward to hear what I have to say?

No, I'm beautiful. That was my wish. And that's fine.

But, oh! To have it all!

The vampire sank, as if he were snorkeling. He slid, and he slithered. He was underwater in some other world. Devnee hung on to the wall, lest he pull her along and drown her.

He said, "You and I, Devnee . . ."

The air was thick and swampy where he stood.

"We do what is necessary, do we not, Devnee?"

William was an honor student and did things like Model United Nations, and High School Bowl, and French Club, and Chess. He was not an athlete but loved sports, and was the announcer for the basketball season, the manager for the baseball season. In music he was the saxophone player who led the Jazz Band and Pit Band.

Devnee struggled to breathe in the mossy air, the wet drowning air.

Her wish glittered in her head, brilliant and bright and full of knowledge. She tried to grab the wish and break it on the floor, like a piece of glass, but instead it shone like a mirror, and she saw herself reflected in it: brilliant and bright and full of knowledge.

And the wish came out of her mouth, and trembled in the room, and became the possession of the vampire.

"I wish I were smart," said Devnee.

But the room was empty.

The vampire had left.

To fulfill the wish.

Chapter 13

Devnee never did paint the tower room. She never did put a carpet on the floor, nor bright curtains over the shutters.

Her mother stayed in the kitchen, happily designing shelves into which the coffeepot and the blender would fit perfectly; her father stayed in the workshop, busily making the little nooks and crannies for the kitchen; her brother stayed at school, playing every conceivable ball game and proving that it does not matter how many state lines you cross — the star athlete can still skip homework.

As for Devnee, she, too, could skip homework.

And get an A-plus doing it.

How delightful it was to sit in class, always having the answer, always getting the point, always catching the teacher's eye and sharing a rueful smile when the other kids were too thick to get the joke.

How strange it was to fill in the blanks without thinking. To write an essay without pondering. To know that your spelling and punctuation were correct. To glance down at the multiple choices and be amused; to spot a little joke on the teacher's part, a joke observed only by the really bright members of the class. To finish the one-hour test in eighteen minutes and spend the rest of the time looking around.

At first Devnee was careful not to look at Victoria.

Victoria had walked in with long demanding strides, daring you to keep up, and despising you if you fell behind. Victoria no longer had the walk. She was just a female thing who slouched from one desk to another, confused and mumbling.

During quizzes Victoria bent over her desk in that hunched desperate way of people who can't think of any solution except to get closer to the paper. Victoria clung to her pencil as if the lead itself might know the answers. She had the tense, frightened look of a little kid on a strange doorstep, wondering if a boogeyman will answer the door.

Well, one had.

Devnee was asked to substitute for Victoria on the High School Bowl team.

This was a group she had heard about, but certainly had never seen in action. Devnee had had difficulty following the strategy of a volleyball game, never mind a sort of young person's *Jeopardy*.

Trey and William were on High School Bowl.

She knew William was brilliant, but had never assessed Trey that way. His rough, hard looks and his swaggering possession of the ground almost hid his brains.

Devnee, Trey, and William sat behind one long table while the opposition sat behind another. A nasal-voiced vice principal from a third school — for objectivity — read aloud questions taken moments before from a sealed envelope.

"What are the basic structural units of proteins?" said the vice principal sternly, as if interrogating enemy troops.

"Amino acids," said Devnee, pushing her buzzer first, and answering instantly.

"Name two types of arthropods."

Easy, thought Devnee. "Arachnids and crustaceans," she said, laughing. She poised her finger over the buzzer for the next question.

Of course they slaughtered the other team.

Devnee scored more than twice as high as anybody else, answering things she had no idea that she knew. It was eerie, not to be acquainted with the interior of her own mind.

Because it's not my mind, thought Devnee. It doesn't even belong to me. I stole it.

Quickly she thought of it in another light.

It's Victoria's own fault. I deserved to be Sweetheart at the dance, and if she'd let me be elected, instead of campaigning for Aryssa, who hardly even exists anymore, let alone deserves to be a dance queen, well, I would have let Victoria keep her brains.

She felt almost generous because, after all, Victoria had had a chance to stay brilliant and blown it.

"In what year and in what city was the second Continental Congress?" said the vice principal.

Devnee had to laugh out loud. Baby questions. "1775, Philadelphia," she said.

How impressed Trey was. "What a dark horse you are, Devnee. I never realized you had such a great background."

A week ago she would not have known what "dark horse" meant; she would have had to ask or else never known, or even — in her dull moments — never wondered. But tonight she knew, of course, that a dark horse was an unexpected, unknown winner in a race.

How right Trey is, thought Devnee. I am a dark horse.

Following a dark path.

They went out afterward to celebrate, of course. The teacher who supervised High School Bowl was Mrs. Cort. "Oh, Devnee, I'm so excited that you moved to town," she said. "We need minds like yours."

Devnee cringed. There was no mind on earth like hers. A stolen mind. What was Victoria's mind now? Dim? Unlit? Confused? Did Devnee have the entire contents of Victoria's mind? Or just the academic facts? Would she one day slide into Victoria's life as well, with Victoria's family and history?

Trey smooched Devnee. The kiss she would have given her soul to get a month ago was nothing. Damp lips bunched up and tapping her cheek. Trey had no idea what he was kissing and didn't care. He wanted only looks.

But so did I, thought Devnee. I wanted only looks. So this is fair.

"And what does your brilliant mind want on its ice-cream sundae?" asked Trey.

Victoria's brains, thought Devnee.

She bit her lip to keep from saying that out loud, covered her mouth with her hand, wondering if the fangs in her mouth . . .

No.

I don't have the fangs. The vampire has the fangs. I must keep my story straight.

"Chocolate, of course, like you," said Devnee. And then, because she could not help herself, "How's Victoria?"

William looked confused, as if when Victoria's mind was emptied, the minds and memories of her friends were also sapped. "She's fine," he said dubiously. "She just . . . I don't know . . . I guess . . . I guess I don't know." He stirred his chocolate sauce into his melting vanilla ice cream. He shrugged. "I'm not really sure what's going on," he said.

"Women," said Trey, dismissing half the race. "They can really be a pain." He grinned at Devnee. "I go by looks, and that spares me the trouble of ever worrying about their problems."

Lovely, thought Devnee. Just the kind of boyfriend we all want.

"I guess Victoria's just in kind of a slump," said William.

"We miss her on the team, of course," said Mrs. Cort briskly. "But life goes on. Now, tomorrow we'll have practice."

The boys moaned.

"You practice for High School Bowl just the way you practice for any other team," said Mrs. Cort firmly.

"Dev doesn't need to practice," said Trey. "She knows it all already."

In the English class where once Mrs. Cort had only had Victoria to call on, Devnee had all the answers, while Victoria was simply dense.

Mrs. Cort loved test questions in which you must know the facts in order to answer, but you don't write the facts down. You write down an independent conclusion. Devnee had always failed these questions.

It was Victoria who did not have to think; Victoria's questing mind would have already probed at the difficulty this aspect of literature presented.

Whereas Devnee would certainly never have thought of it before and would be completely flummoxed having to think of it now.

But things were different.

Now it was Victoria whose mind didn't lead anywhere. Just sat at the desk, thick and uncertain. It was Victoria who nervously bit a lock of hair and nervously drummed a pencil eraser, and nervously stared at the wall clock and then her wristwatch.

Is that how I used to look? thought Devnee. Pathetic? Hopeless?

She could not bear the sight of Victoria. You could actually see Victoria's mind scrabbling for facts, like a falling mountain climber scrabbling for a crack in the rock.

A dreadful taste coated Devnee's mouth.

A queer moldy glaze coated her eyes.

Victoria ran out of energy. She lay down her pencil, turned her test over, and put her head on the desk, eyes not closed, but soul not looking out, either. Just dim staring.

What have I done? thought Devnee Fountain.

Her mind skipped on without her: Victoria's mind, actually; a mind redolent of intriguing observation and complete knowledge. Thoughts so amusing they begged to be shared with the class. Intelligence so excellent it demanded a pencil, so she could write down her conclusions.

Inside the new body, isolated from the new mind, Devnee herself sat very still. I never knew the real Devnee, she thought, and now I'm not going to. I'm going to be pieces of other girls instead.

Sunlight poured in the side windows and the

shadows, as clear as drawings, of the students were outlined against the walls: silhouettes of pencils poised and heads bowed in thought.

Only Devnee cast no shadow.

She stared at the blank wall.

My shadow hates me, thought Devnee. The vampire lied. It isn't that my shadow doesn't like to be around when the event occurs. It's that my shadow doesn't want to be around somebody like me.

Somebody whose wishes destroy other people.

Devnee had a hideously clear view of herself, as if she had turned to ice, and all the inessentials were chipped away.

She was bad.

Event. What a ridiculous word. Those were not "events" — those moments that destroyed Aryssa and Victoria. Those were betrayals: the selling of friends to evil.

But it is not possible to look at oneself for long. The sight is too dreadful. So Devnee quickly looked away.

At the end of class, to remind herself of why she had done it, she stopped in at the girls' room, where a row of six mirrors awaited the desperate reflections of desperate girls.

It was delightful to stand at a distance. Smiling. Knowing her hair was perfect, knowing she was perfect. Pitying the stubby, faded girls who leaned up close to the mirrors, repairing or changing faces and hair, in a futile effort to have what Devnee had.

One of the girls was Aryssa.

What happened to Aryssa is not my fault, Devnee reminded herself. How was I to know he was a vampire? It was just a wish. A plain old wish. Lots of girls wish to be beautiful. How could I know it would really come true?

Stolen beauty is not like stolen jewelry. There's no prison sentence, no time in jail. The police can't catch me.

Aryssa was looking at Devnee. Her lusterless eyes were seeking answers. Large eyes, those of a waif in the gutter, hoping for handouts. The eyes of Aryssa came to rest on Devnee.

She knows I did it, Devnee thought. Her heart went into spasms.

But Aryssa said, "Hi, Devnee. Are we still buddies? I kind of forget. I've been having a bad time lately. I'm sorry I haven't kept in touch."

Devnee flinched and drew away. Bumped into Victoria. Not a leader now, but merely somebody in the line.

It was remarkable how her personality had been sapped. She was even more of a husk than Aryssa; when Victoria's demanding presence collapsed, there was not much left.

"I love how you do your hair," said an unknown girl to Devnee. "I mean, you look so perfect all the time. I wish I looked like you."

Two other girls turned away from the mirror, also, and smiled at Devnee. "You should go into modeling," said one of them. "My sister is a model. But you'd be even better."

"You have the bones for it," agreed the first girl.

Devnee turned her back on the remains of Aryssa and Victoria.

Chapter 14

Devnee was not a particular fan of television, being too attached to her radio to turn on the TV. Devnee had three stations from which she continually switched. One was soft old-fashioned rock, beginner rock, so to speak. The next station was current rock, but not the kind that got parents up in arms. The final station was country, where the lyrics told sad stories and the rhymes were like greeting cards.

She loved them equally. She could not bear talk shows, or advertising, or news.

Her mother, however, loved a local station full of friendly local weather idiots, and giggling local celebrities, and dim local thinkers.

Devnee came home from another day of triumph and beauty to find her mother swaying in the kitchen to the beat of a local department store jingle. Really, how pathetic, thought Devnee. This is the best I can do for a mother? A mother whose radio station plays bingo and describes spaghetti suppers at the firehouse? Please.

I deserve better than this.

"Hello, darling," said her mother, kissing her swiftly. "Tell me what you think of this wallpaper for the breakfast room."

"It's perfect," said Devnee, not looking.

"Here are two possibilities, Devnee. Help me choose."

"Mom, you have a great eye for color. Whatever you choose is perfect."

"Come on, Devvy," said her mother, pulling out the old baby name.

"Ma."

"Dance with me," said her mother, pulling out the old baby after-school activity.

"Ma!"

Her mother deflated. She stepped away and looked sadly at the wallpaper samples, as if she had expected great things to come from them; as if she had expected to transform both the wall and her life and perhaps also her relationship with her daughter.

Her mother stared out the kitchen window. The backyard was grim and wintry, and the hemlocks were like a dark green prison wall. No sky, no town, no neighbor was visible.

"I don't know, Devvy," said her mother sadly. "You are a different person since we moved here."

Devnee had decided several days ago to stop

thinking about the differences. It just gave her an upset stomach. The point of life was to be beautiful and have fun. She was not going to think of the techniques used to arrive there.

"I can feel you full of wishes," said her mother. "Wishing to be somebody else. To be somewhere else. Wishing you had a different family."

The truth stung. Devnee must not let her mother see any more of it. She rallied. "I like the wallpaper with the ribbon effect, Mom. I think your watercolors would look terrific against it."

Her mother continued to study the hemlocks. She frowned slightly, tilted her head, and looked more intently.

"I don't even feel as if I recognize you these days," said her mother with infinite sadness.

"I'm just wearing my hair differently," said Devnee casually.

Her mother nodded. "I love it like that. You're beautiful, sweetheart. I love looking at you. But — Devvy, you don't even talk the way you used to! What's going on? Tell me. Please."

"I'm just learning to manage my study time better, Mother. Aren't you proud of me?"

A shadow crossed her mother's face. She fiddled with the wallpaper samples. She tilted her body, looking out the window again, toward the hemlocks. Devnee followed her gaze.

Caught in the hemlocks like an immense moth was the vampire's cloak.

"There's something . . ." Her mother's voice

trailed off. "I can't quite focus on it. My perspective is off. There's — I don't know — it looks like — I think it's dirty laundry stuck on the tree."

Only her mother would look at a vampire's cloak and see laundry. Her mother was probably even now thinking of bleach and detergent; probably even now making the kind of pitiful plans that filled her day: *I'll just go out there and get that; run a load of laundry and have it all nice and sparkly clean and freshly white.*

Pathetic, thought Devnee. I wish I had a different mother.

The wish went right out the window, fluttering toward the hemlocks.

A different mother, thought Devnee.

Her heart stopped. Her tongued thickened.

She looked with horror at the woman standing in her kitchen: a happy woman, who liked her life and her family. Who loved her daughter.

"No," said Devnee. "No!" And then much louder, *"No! I didn't mean it!"*

Her mother did not seem to have heard. She moved toward the back door. Put her hand on the knob.

"No," said Devnee, "don't go out there, Mom. You stay inside. You — listen, I love this wallpaper. I'll go out there and get that thing off the hemlocks and you — um — well, let's go to the wallpaper store together! Huh? Won't that be fun?"

"Really? Would you like to?" said her mother. "Maybe while we're there we can look at paper for the tower. I know you love it the way it is, Devvy, but somehow when I'm up there alone, it feels dark to me."

Devnee's laugh was hysterical. "Don't go there alone, Mom, okay? I keep my room clean. You don't need to go there."

Her mother was still frowning, still confused. "I don't know, Devvy, there's so much about this house. . . . Sometimes in the day I feel as if I'm not alone. . . . Sometimes I even seem to hear someone laughing."

It was Devnee who was laughing now. Horrible little bursts of insane hysterical laughter spurted out of her.

Her mother shuddered. "Just like that, Devvy. Don't laugh like that. It makes me so nervous."

Devnee stopped laughing, as if she'd sliced off her laugh with a machete. "I'll be right back, Mom," she said. "You stay here where it's warm. Promise?"

Her mother was getting her jacket. Getting her gloves.

"Mom," said Devnee, "let's have a cup of tea. You put the water on to boil. I'll have apple mint, okay? We haven't had a cup of tea together in weeks." She put her mother's jacket back. Stuck the tea kettle in her mother's hand.

Wild distant laughter pealed. Mother and daughter swung toward the kitchen window and saw hemlocks shaking, as if the heavy green branches were crackling with fire.

How dare that sick, twisted, perverted vampire try to get near her mother! Devnee would kill him!

"Wait here," she said sternly to her mother, and she stormed out the back door, strode over the dead grass of winter, marched to the hemlocks, and grabbed hold of the cloak.

"Don't you dare go near my mother," said Devnee Fountain.

The vampire's teeth appeared, loose in the trees, a fang here, a fang there. "I believe you made a wish."

"I take it back. I wasn't thinking."

"Pity," said the vampire. "I'm afraid it's still a wish."

"You scum!" spat Devnee. "How dare you!"

"I'm afraid," said the vampire, "I cannot quite follow your distinctions. Why was it fine to wish for Aryssa's beauty and Victoria's brains, but not fine to wish for a different mother? I think you deserve a better mother, too."

"This is the one I have!" said Devnee.

"That was the body you had," pointed out the vampire, "and the mind. You wouldn't settle for them. Why settle for a pathetic excuse of a mother? Other girls have mothers who are successful attorneys, or brilliant novelists, or creative designers."

"I'm keeping my own mother."

"Mmmmm. The wish, however, my dear. The wish is here, you know. I possess it. It was a very complete wish. I was in your mind at the time, and

I saw quite clearly the kind of mother you would prefer."

"You did not! I prefer my mother!" Devnee yanked at the cape and sure enough, a piece of it came off in her hands. But it was not cloth. It was some sort of moss, and in the heat of her hands it melted into algae, into scum, and stained her hand green. She wiped her hands on her jeans and stained the jeans. "Get off me!" she shouted.

"I'm *in* you," he said.

"I don't want this! You can't have her! I take it back! Go away! Take your cloak and go!"

He shook his head. His trunk, his cape, and his trees shook with him, swaying back and forth like some encapsulated inland gale. "You opened my shutters. You let me in. You sent me wishes. You presented me with your shadow."

"No."

"What do you mean — no? You can't change your mind in the middle of your transformation, Devnee. You wanted it all, and you're getting it all. You will be perfect. You will have beauty and brains and money and talent . . . and an interesting mother worthy of such a daughter."

"I will blot you off the landscape if you touch my mother."

He vanished.

Ha! thought Devnee, triumphant.

But instead, the voice of the vampire came through the bottoms of her feet. She cried out and lifted first one foot and then the other, but she could not lift them both at the same time, and the vampire oozed through her soles and into her body and up, up, up into her mind.

Blot away your beauty, too?

Blot away your brains?

I doubt that, Devnee. There will be no blotting. Because your real wish, your real first wish, Devnee, your real wish was to have it all.

Have it all.

That means more, my dear.

More, and more, and more.

"I don't want it now," she said. She was very, very cold. The stain on her hand hurt like a burn, and the stain on her jeans stank like a swamp.

"Please?" she said. She was crying now, and the tears hurt even more than the stains; they seemed to be cutting trenches in her face; she would have scars from her eyes to her chin; where the tears hit the ground there would be pits eaten away from the acid that was Devnee.

"Please don't hurt my mother," she said brokenly.

"Well . . ." said the vampire. "I am willing to postpone your mother."

"Fine," said Devnee. "Anything."

His smile was immense. His fangs were all around her now, like some gruesome winter wreath: icicles closing in on her neck.

"I have certainly enjoyed Aryssa and Victoria," said the vampire. "But there is a girl my eye keeps going to. Her name is Karen."

"I don't remember a Karen," said Devnee dully.

"No? She's in your gym class. She's the one who's so excellent in sports."

Now Devnee remembered. She didn't much care for athletes. Karen was sweaty and musclebound. She was always dribbling a basketball or doing backbends. Devnee herself loathed games. Gang showers. Sweat. Coaches. And most of all basketball. Devnee could never remember which end of the court was her basket. In gym, people despised her.

Perhaps only gym is where I'm still real, she thought. In gym, I show.

His teeth came out again: long and thin and very slick, for puncturing without slowing down.

His laugh was the sound of a car that will not start on a winter morning: grinding, dead, batteryless.

"Karen," he said.

She closed her eyes.

What had Karen done to deserve this? Karen had never even spoken to Devnee!

"No, I can't," said Devnee. "I've done this enough. I —"

"Fine. I accept your mother."

Devnee's tears rolled to the edges of her mouth and there they tasted not of salt but of blood.

"I'm a little out of control," said the vampire. "I'm so hungry, you see. All this chatter has whetted my appetite. I want more. Just like you, Devnee, darling."

144

"All right," she whispered. "Karen."

"Tomorrow," he said.

"Tomorrow," she said.

The vampire vanished.

Devnee staggered back to the house. The tea was steeped and waiting. Her mother had heated a cinnamon coffee cake she had made that morning. The kitchen smelled of love.

"What was it?" asked her mother.

"Nothing. Some old piece of plastic that blew into the yard. I threw it in the trash."

"Thank you, darling." Her mother set the cup of tea before her. Steam rose up from the tea cup and Devnee thought of evil genies rising out of Egyptian urns. What had risen in this house?

What had she, Devnee Fountain, given permission to?

From across the table, her mother blew Devnee a kiss.

The kiss was visible: as clear on the air as a leaf falling. And fall it did. The kiss did not reach Devnee. It fell in the middle of the table, between the sugar and the lemons.

She tried to pick it up, but it broke in her hand.

She was no longer human. Even kisses could not touch her now.

Chapter 15

After school, Victoria burst into tears. "My parents are really on my case!" she said. "My grades have fallen and I don't have any energy and they're so mad at me."

Devnee could hardly bear to look at Victoria. But she forced herself to examine the girl. Lost was Victoria's athlete-breaking-the-ribbon look. Now, she more closely resembled the torn and frayed ribbon itself.

My mother could be next, thought Devnee. *My mother.*

"That's rough, Victoria," said one of the other girls.

How unnoticing they were. Victoria's problems hardly skimmed the surface of their day. How absorbed each girl was by her own existence, how selfish about others.

Selfish! thought Devnee. I am actually annoyed with the rest for being selfish? I — who caused this collapse?

"I don't know what to do," wept Victoria. She was wilted, like a flower that had once been a proud tulip and was now just a broken stem.

I never thought of Victoria as a real person, thought Devnee. I never thought of Victoria as having parents and problems, or even *life*. I pretended she was just an object, and I could have part of her.

William gave Victoria a hug. "You'll feel better in a few days," he promised, as if he could control it.

Devnee knew otherwise. It was, after all, her own wish, but she could not control it, either.

Or can I?

Can I gain control?

Devnee straightened, firmed, drew herself in.

He wants Karen. But what he actually said was: He would postpone having my mother. But he does not seem to be able to go out and get victims on his own. He has to have a conduit. He needs to have somebody like me to open his dark path.

I can't give him another girl. I can't give him Karen.

But if I don't give him Karen, my mother is right in the house with him! The path is surely already open. What if my mother went into my room to straighten up? What if my mother decided suddenly to wash windows in the tower?

That sounded like her mother.

What then? Where would the dark path go?

Victoria dried her tears, but she did not look

done with crying. "I feel as if somebody scooped me out."

Devnee almost screamed. She had a vision of the vampire with an ice-cream scoop, taking this and that out of Victoria's head, and leaving her with pits and holes instead.

"You probably have mono," diagnosed William.

"No. I'm brain-dead."

No, no, no, no, thought Devnee. No, I didn't wish for that! I wished for brains, but surely, surely, I didn't really wish to destroy Victoria to get them. Did I? Please, please, tell me I didn't wish to hurt anybody like this.

"How can you tell?" said William gently.

"I'm failing every class," cried Victoria. "Good clue, huh?"

William's hug turned to comfort. "I love you anyway," he said.

How nice William was. How rare the quality of niceness had turned out to be. Plenty of people had beauty, plenty of people had brains, plenty of people had money — but who in this immense school, with its huge student body, had turned out to be just plain nice? Certainly not Devnee Fountain.

I should have wished for that. To be nice.

The wish teased along the edges of her mind and thoughts. If she were nice, as well as beautiful and brilliant . . . why, she would —

There was a softening of her skull. A weakening

of her brain. A feeling of wind through her ears. The vampire was within a step of her thoughts.

He comes in when I let him! thought Devnee. I thought he could come of his own accord, but he can't. I actually open the door myself: I wish for anything — and he comes in.

She drew her thoughts and her soul together and removed any wishes, stalled any yearning. Even for being nice. For anything at all. She grew hard and solid, like concrete bunkers.

The vampire was gone before he had quite gotten in. He was not able to converse with her on the inside of her head, the way he had in the past. She had kicked him out.

Pulses of triumph rocked her body; she throbbed with power.

"I can't stand girls who whine," said Trey, muttering about Victoria. He frowned at the way William was holding her, as if to offer comfort were to break the rules. "Jeez," he added. He sighed heavily, burdened by the mere presence of a girl who whined.

I sold out for him? Devnee thought.

No, I sold out for beauty. But I needed the beauty to attract a Trey. To make friends. I love my beauty. I don't want to give it up. It's absolutely wonderful being beautiful.

But it doesn't make a selfish hunk into a nice boy.

I wish —

Across the lobby the shadows shifted and became a single line and oozed slowly over the glittering marble toward Devnee.

I don't wish!

She had caught it in time, slashing off the edge of the wish before the dark path could gather speed.

But if I foil him . . . If I don't surrender again and give him Karen . . . what position will that place my own mother in? And we're not moving! That's our house! We're stuck! We're all stuck. My mother, my father, my brother, me . . . and the vampire.

There is no way out.

And the vampire knows it.

"Hi, Devnee," said an unfamiliar voice.

Devnee looked up. She felt as if a plate of translucent glass had been dropped between herself and the world: She could see the shapes, but not the people. Because I don't want them to be people, she thought with horror. I want them to be body parts that I steal.

"Karen," said the unfamiliar voice, reminding Devnee.

A gurgle of sickness rose up in Devnee's throat and she fought it down. Weakness could no longer be allowed. "Hi, Karen," she said brightly. "How are you? What's happening? Did you just come from practice?"

Karen was damp from a gym shower. Not a pretty girl, Karen had personality — armloads of it: She seemed to vibrate behind that sheet of unclear glass with friendship and other good things.

Good things waiting to be destroyed, thought Devnee. What could be worse for a dedicated athlete than a vampire's visit?

Visit.

Who am I kidding here?

Let's say it plainly, Devnee Fountain, and make yourself realize what is actually going on. Admit the truth. You turned Aryssa and Victoria over to a subhuman beast who sucked their blood for his lunch. A beast whose next victims will be innocent Karen and your very own mother.

Devnee looked down, hugging herself, trying to pull herself together, to think of a way out of this mess. She was wearing a very short skirt and a shirt with the sleeves partly rolled up. Her ivory satin skin glowed.

Aryssa's skin, really.

Devnee gagged and swallowed hard. She had the feeling she could unzip herself and step out. Leave Aryssa's skin lying on the lobby floor, while the real Devnee — the plain, dull Devnee — would go on as she had before: unnoticed, unloved, unwanted.

Give up my beauty? thought Devnee.

Brilliant thoughts swirled in her head; quotations from Shakespeare and the Bible and Lincoln were complete and meaningful behind her eyes.

Victoria's thoughts and quotations.

Give up my brain? thought Devnee.

If I give up my beauty, my father won't be proud of me anymore. My brother won't brag about me to his friends. I won't have any friends. Looking in a mirror and putting on clothes will be just as depressing as it used to be. If I give up my brains, I won't be with William and Trey on High School Bowl. Mrs. Cort won't fawn over me. I'll be that ordinary girl nobody notices, nobody cares about, nobody wants.

She had begun to cry, but she could not feel the tears on her cheeks.

Because it's Aryssa's skin, thought Devnee. Perhaps Aryssa feels the tears, because she's inside *my* skin.

"Dev?" said a gentle voice. "What's wrong? Tell me."

Devnee opened her eyes. It was Victoria.

"You seem so down," said Victoria. "What's wrong?"

Devnee laughed hysterically.

Victoria said, "Believe me, I know how it feels to have a bad day. About all I seem to be able to do this week is get out of bed. I have dried leaves for a brain. Lots of rustling around when the wind goes through my head."

Dried leaves rustling in her head did not have to come from emptiness. It could come from the presence of the vampire. Sometimes his very laughter sounded like the cruel rasping of branches in winter.

"Maybe you'll feel better next week," said Devnee. But she did not know if the victims got better in the end, or if they stayed tired and worn and too exhausted to function. Even if Victoria isn't tired next week, thought Devnee, she'll still be dumb. Even if Aryssa isn't tired next week, she'll still be plain.

"I hope so," agreed Victoria. "Maybe it's just a stage. But what's happening with you, Dev? To make you so sad?" Victoria was truly concerned. She had left William's side and come over to ask.

I had three assigned buddies, thought Devnee. Aryssa, whom I gave to a vampire; Trey, who is a hunk but conceited and shallow; Nina, who is nothing more than a checkbook.

But Victoria really is a buddy.

If she knew . . .

If anybody knew . . .

"I'm not a very nice person," said Devnee Fountain. That was the wish she should have made: to be nice.

The very word *wish,* even when she was not making a wish, was terribly dangerous. Across the lobby the dark path began again to ooze forward, so it could arrive at the intersection of his victims.

No! thought Devnee. I cannot let this happen! "I have to go to my locker. Come on and talk to me while we go." Swiftly she linked one arm with Karen and the other with Victoria and trotted them out of the lobby.

School had ended some time ago.

Even the late buses were long gone. Sports

practice was over. Tutoring had ended. The custodians had turned off most of the hall lights.

Light came only from behind, from the lobby.

Long black shadows, much much taller than the girls, trotted on ahead, as if scouting out the territory. *Three shadows. For three girls.*

My shadow is back! thought Devnee. My shadow forgave me. My shadow thinks there's a chance that maybe I can be human after all.

"Gosh, Devnee," said Karen, "thanks for including me."

"Sure," said Devnee, rushing them on, turning the corner, leaving the dark path behind.

Devnee was the kind of nonathlete whose stumbling stupidity caused any team she might be on to lose any game it might play. Victoria was fairly good at sports that required time and money, but not teamwork, like horseback riding and skiing. Karen, however, was a superstar among athletes and, in a year or two, would be recruited by college coaches with big plans. Devnee, Victoria, and Karen were not a likely trio.

But Karen did not appear to notice.

"Let's — um — go get a doughnut," said Devnee. "Want to go to the Hole and have doughnuts?"

None of them had a car.

"We'll have to catch the boys if we're going to go," mumbled Victoria. "I wish I had some strength. I can hardly make my feet shuffle. You'll have to order my doughnut for me."

"This is so nice of you," Karen said. "I'm new in town, too. I feel so special that you're asking me to go with you."

Devnee had had no idea that Karen was new in town. Karen seemed so established.

"I hardly have any friends yet," confided Karen. "I got on all the teams without any trouble, and we're buddies, and I have a good time, and yet I don't really have friends. You know what I mean?"

"I know what you mean," said Devnee.

Karen beamed at Devnee. Happiness transformed her. She was suddenly beautiful.

Beauty, thought Devnee. I don't even know what it is anymore.

Karen's smile demanded a smile in return. When Devnee's beautiful borrowed face broke into a real smile, some of her inhumanity dissolved. Some of the real Devnee surfaced.

And thinking occurred.

Real thinking.

Not the stolen thoughts out of Victoria's brain, not quotes, not formulas and facts.

Genuine shrewd planning and strategies.

I won't give him Karen. I didn't make a wish anyway, so he can't have Karen, no matter how much he wants her. He can't have anybody if I don't turn them over, can he? They have to be part of my wish, don't they? Karen isn't. So he can't have Karen.

I did make a terrible wish about my family,

back at the beginning of all this. Even my mother felt the truth about that wish. He half possesses that wish.

I am calling it back.

He cannot have that wish.

Somehow — some way — using what weapon I don't know — paying what price I don't know — I have to stop him.

Stop him forever.

And return what I stole to the rightful owners.

She looked behind.

The corner, dim and distant, blackened.

The dark path crawled around the lockers.

Laughter like a million breaking souls crept along the floor.

She could see the edge of the cape now, and smell the rising swamp gas of his shadow.

"Quick," said Devnee Fountain, pushing Victoria and Karen ahead of her. "Outside. We'll meet the boys there."

They ran because she made them.

Behind her, the dark path oozed on.

But ahead of her, equally dark, attached to her feet the way it ought to be, spread her own shadow, huge and threatening in the setting sun.

Chapter 16

In High School Bowl practice Devnee asked the only question that really mattered. "How do you kill a vampire?" she said.

Nobody blinked an eye. They were used to an assortment of study topics from chemistry to famous dancers, so the subject of how to off a vampire seemed normal.

"I am not sure," said Mrs. Cort, with a frown of uncertainty. "I believe it's necessary to put a stake through its heart."

Trey said, "You carry a cross when you do it."

"And chew garlic," added William.

Devnee had not expected any of these answers. "Have you had experience with this?" she said.

"No," said Trey, "but that's why houses lots of times have wooden doors with crosses on them."

Devnee wasn't certain if she had ever seen a door with a cross on it.

"Wood molding," explained William, "in the

shape of a big T. Or cross. That way, the vampire can't get in the door."

Devnee's mouth fell open. Trey laughed at her.

Mrs. Cort stuck to the ever-essential subject of High School Bowl questions. "Every now and then they do ask questions on superstition and myth. Where is Transylvania, what is voodoo, which mummies escaped their tombs, who wrote *Dr. Jekyll and Mr. Hyde.*"

Superstition and myth, thought Devnee. I should be so lucky that he is nothing more than superstition and myth.

She felt the vampire tapping at her skull and did not let him in. Force of mind could keep him out of her thoughts. It was only when she weakened, lowered her guard, or had wishes and yearnings and aches for things to be different — only then could the vampire come in.

There was nothing now that Devnee wanted except to be free of him, and have her mother be safe.

Not much, she thought, oh, no, not much.

Just life and breath and family.

Well, she did not think much of the suggestions of the High School Bowl team. Chew garlic? Please. The vampire stank of swamps and putrid gas already. He wouldn't even notice garlic. Wear a cross? That was possible. But Devnee felt she should not stand behind the symbol of a god she had not trusted. She had not asked God for beauty and brains. She had asked the vampire. It would be slimy now, wouldn't it, to back up and say, Well, I really believed in you all the time, gimme your cross, take care of me.

And as for the stake through the heart — why, most of the time the vampire's body wasn't even there. And his body had no heart; it was the collected shadows of the dead, wrapped in his evil cloak.

"Trey?"

"Yeah?"

"Remember you mentioned a creepy girl used to live in my house?"

Trey and William both shuddered. "Whew, was she ever weird," said Trey.

No wonder she was weird, thought Devnee. I'm feeling pretty weird myself. "What happened to her?"

The boys shrugged. "She just disappeared one day. She used to date a guy in this school. He graduated. Her parties were legend. Everybody wanted to go up into that tower, and she would never let them." Trey laughed. "She told her boyfriend that the shutters were haunted."

William laughed, too. "I remember that now. If she'd said her house was haunted, or her tower — you could believe that. It's such a spooky house. But shutters? Did ghosts live in the slats?"

There was space between the two sets of shutters. Was that the vampire's tomb? A tomb of darkness on the inside and light on the outside? A tomb with access to towers and skies? A tomb from which shadows cast long black paths?

"What was her name?" said Devnee.

Nobody could remember the creepy girl's name.

"Do you guys ever go up into the tower?" William wanted to know.

"It's my bedroom."

"No kidding! *You sleep there?*" William put a middle finger into his mouth for gagging on.

Devnee managed a laugh. "My bed is up there. But no, nobody could sleep there. Too much going on, what with the ghosts and the haunts and the banging shutters and the vampires. I get very little rest."

The boys smiled, and Mrs. Cort dragged out another set of quiz questions. French history. Talleyrand and Mitterand, Charlemagne and Charles de Gaulle. Devnee, of course, knew them all. "What famous building did the people of Paris destroy at the beginning of the French Revolution?" said Mrs. Cort.

"The Bastille," said Devnee. This is what it would be like, she thought, if they substituted computers for brains. You would know how to pronounce it and spell it, what it looks like, the date it came down. You would spew out the answer like a laser printer. But it wouldn't be yours. It would be the computer's. I want to put the facts inside my brain by myself. I want to give Victoria back her mind.

Devnee faced the fact that she did not want to give Aryssa back her beauty.

Either I take the vampire's evil gifts or I don't, she thought. I can't decide that half of it's evil and the other half is nice and I'm hanging on to it.

She wondered what the poor creepy girl had given to, or taken from, the vampire. And where was she now? Safe and well? Or one of the shadows beneath his cloak? Was the cloak filled by the shadows of girls like Devnee, who once had taken the bus, done homework, gone to basketball games . . . and made a fatal wish?

There would be no more wishes for Devnee Fountain.

She would never use the word again.

"What famous edifice in Paris was erected for a World's Fair?" said Mrs. Cort.

"The Eiffel Tower," said William.

The three team members smiled at one another. They were good.

"I hope we win over Durham High," said Trey. "They whipped us last time. I can't stand being whipped."

"I think we will," said William. "Devnee was fabulous against Roosevelt High."

"I know we will," said Mrs. Cort. "Between the three of you, you seem to have everything covered."

In another life, at another time, Devnee would have spoken out loud, adding her own thought. Devnee's sentence would have begun with two words she was determined never to touch again: *I wish* we would win.

What a contrast to the others. They hoped, or thought, or knew. They didn't wish.

Be careful of wishes, thought Devnee.

They might come true.

Chapter 17

Devnee entered the house with a spring in her step.

She felt not just beautiful and not just brilliant, but also strong and clever and tough.

She bounded into the big front hall.

"Mom?" she called.

There was no answer.

The house seemed much darker inside than usual.

Devnee stood very still.

"Mom?"

The house filled with faint sound. Fluttering here, rasping there, creaking above, and hissing below.

"Mom!" shouted Devnee.

Her mother's voice was soft as a flute. "I'm in the tower, darling."

Devnee took the stairs two at a time.

Halfway up, she smothered in a tapestry of black. Choking, pushing it away from her face, she kicked at it. It swirled around her legs, caught her hair, tilted her head back as if to strangle her. "Trying to back out?" said the vampire.

His cloak was ice water, lowering her temperature, lowering her resistance.

"Trying to retreat?" said the vampire.

His glass eyeballs were not in their sockets. His fingernails were not on his hands. His parts shifted and slithered and stank.

"Mom!" screamed Devnee.

"I'm up here, darling. I made the loveliest wish. And it came true."

The vampire's giggle was like bubbles underwater. She had the sense that she could bottle him, like seltzer, swamp-flavored. I'm going to be hysterical, thought Devnee. I can't fall apart. Not now.

"Mom. Come downstairs. Now."

Her mother did not answer.

Devnee's own shadow melded with the shadows in the vampire's cloak. She could not tell where hers left off and his began. "Give me back my shadow," she cried.

"There is no giving or taking with a shadow," said the vampire. "There is merely light and dark. Your shadow seems to be part of the dark, my dear. You have lost it. And shortly, very shortly, your mother will lose hers."

"No, she won't! You can't! Stop this! She's my mother!"

"Victoria has a mother. Aryssa has a mother. You didn't seem to worry about them. I don't quite see the difference."

"I was wrong," whispered Devnee. "I'm sorry. Please undo it. Take back the beauty. Take back the brains. Let me have my mother, please."

"You'll have your mother, my dear. She'll just be . . . a little different."

"What did she wish for?" screamed Devnee, hand over her mouth. I don't want my mother any different, she thought. I love my mother the way she is.

"That's not what you said before," the vampire told her. "I distinctly recall how fervently you wished for a better family. More interesting. Slender. Attractive. Socially acceptable."

"I was wrong. I didn't mean it."

"You did mean it," said the vampire, and he was right. Devnee knew he was right. She had meant it; she had made the wish; the wish had been strong.

"I learned a lesson," said Devnee desperately.

"Human beings always do," agreed the vampire. "Just a little late, that's all." He smiled, and the smile grew from a tiny piece of pleasure to a great gaping cave of fangs and dripping eagerness.

"Not my mother," pleaded Devnee.

The vampire did not speak again. His cloak swirled, closing in on him like a container. If only she could rope him, handcuff him, smash him! But the wind tunnel of his leaving sent her staggering backward down the stairs, struggling just to breathe, let alone fight.

He faded before her eyes, and when the door to the tower stairs opened, there was no hand on the knob, no steps on the treads, no cloak wafting in the air.

She backed up because she had to.

She ran into the kitchen. Of course there was no garlic — her parents did not like garlic. There were no stakes — why would you have a stake in the kitchen?

But there was a door, a door with a cross: the powder room door.

It was on two hinges: pins stuck down shafts. She tried to remove the pins but they did not budge. She tried to jerk the door off anyway but accomplished nothing. She ran back into the kitchen. Found the tool boxes. People who were remodeling had tools everywhere. Grabbed a screwdriver and a hammer. Raced back to the door, sticking the pointed end of the screwdriver on the bottom of the pin and hammering upside down to get the pin out. It was awkward, it was difficult, it took so long! How long would the vampire take to . . .

She could not bear to think of it.

Not her mother!

At last, the pin came out. The door hung stupidly on one hinge.

She got the other pin out. The door fell on her, and it was solid wood, and heavy. So heavy.

How can I ever carry this? thought Devnee. Up two flights of stairs?

Sobbing, she staggered through the kitchen and into the hall, dragging the door after her.

It has to go ahead of me, she thought. The cross has to break through.

But it was too much for her to lift.

What am I doing? she thought, tears spattering her cheeks.

"Mom!" she screamed. "Are you all right?"

There was no answer. There was nothing at all. The silence of the house was as complete as death.

I wish — thought Devnee, and made a dying whimpering sound. I *don't* wish. I — I —

She clung to the edges of the door.

No wishes. *I am.* I do not *wish* to be strong. I *am* strong.

She lifted the door. She balanced it, tilted it, and somehow, pointing it like a ship's prow, got it up the first set of stairs. No velvet cloak blocked the way, no smothering swamp air suffocated her. She stood the door up on its end and opened the tower door. She was panting and sweating. The door weighed as much as an SUV.

One more flight, she said to herself. Then I'll be there.

She went up, pressing her body against the right wall and sliding the door along the left.

She came out into the tower.

Sunlight streamed in every window.

Shutters, yellow with fresh paint, gleamed like love.

Carpet cut into a circle lay like a fluffy lemon on the floor.

"Mom?" whispered Devnee. "Mom, where are you?"

"Right behind you," said her mother. "My goodness, darling, what are you doing with a door?"

Devnee whirled, almost dropping the door. Her mother was standing by the back wall, in white work pants and sweatshirt. She was holding a big can of plaster and with a flat trowel was filling in the cracks on the inner walls.

"I wished," said her mother, before Devnee could stop her, "for good weather."

"That's it?" said Devnee. "That's your wish?"

Her mother smiled. Same old smile. Same old face. Same old pudgy huggy body. "What else is there?" said her mother. "I have the best family and the most interesting house in the world."

Devnee sighed very very deeply. Then she sighed again.

"Why the door?" said her mother again.

"I wanted the door with the cross on it," said Devnee.

Her mother nodded. "Keeps vampires out. Good idea."

Devnee stared. *"Keeps vampires out?"*

Her mother giggled. "You can never be too careful, Devvy. Listen. I just heard Luke come in. Let's all have hot chocolate and brownies." Her mother set down the plaster and the trowel and wiped her hands on her pants. "I'll go heat up the milk," she said, "while you hang your door."

Her mother clattered down the stairs.

Devnee looked around the tower.

It was all light, all sun, all diamonds and freshness.

There was no trace of things dark and cruel.

She did not exchange doors. She leaned the cross door up against the shutters. Even though it blocked some of the sun, the tower stayed cheery and warm.

I'm not sure I needed the cross, she thought. I just needed character. I was weak. I thought somebody had to give me things, or I had to take them away from the people who owned them. Now I'm strong. I know I have to get things myself. Not wish.

He cannot come where wishes do not whisper.

No more whispering for me.

"I am Devnee Fountain," said Devnee out loud. "I am strong. And I am also sorry. I am going to try to give back what I stole."

She looked at her feet. Yes. The sun that came in the window cast a shadow behind her, where it belonged; the outlines of the shadow were firm and clear. But there was no substance to the shadow; it was nothing a vampire could collect; it was just part of her. Mom's right, thought Devnee. The only thing to wish for is lovely weather.

She opened one of the windows and leaned out. It was cold, but crisp and healthy. "Aryssa!" she yelled. "Victoria!"

She filled her lungs with good clean air. "ARYSSA! VICTORIA!"

The vampire had said that human beings learned their lessons — but too late.

Was it too late to return what she had stolen from Aryssa and Victoria?

"It's here!" shouted Devnee. "It's yours! Ask for it! Hope for it! Demand it! Take it!" Just don't wish for it, she thought, and she was laughing, and the laugh was sweet and generous, and if there was any dark path in the yard around the mansion, it was dissolved by Devnee's laugh.

"Dev!" yelled her brother. "Come on. Chocolate's hot!"

She did not look in the mirror as she left the room.

Being beautiful or being ordinary no longer mattered the way it had. What mattered was that she was Devnee Fountain, and her family was wonderful, and her house was interesting.

Down the stairs she clattered.

How ordinary were the sounds of her house! Her mother's voice, her brother's chair scraping, a spoon banging on a pot.

That's what's beautiful, thought Devnee. Ordinary things.

She danced into the kitchen. Her mother had put Marshmallow Fluff on the hot chocolate. Devnee loved Fluff. Life with Fluff was good. Fluff stuck to her lips and she licked at it.

"You look like a dork," said her brother affectionately.

Devnee laughed.

"She does look different," agreed her mother. Mother and brother studied Devnee, heads tilted, struggling to analyze.

"You look happy," said her mother.

I don't have beauty, thought Devnee, feeling it leave, feeling it returning to Aryssa, who needed it so much more. I don't have brains, thought Devnee, feeling that leave, returning to Victoria, who had been kind even without it.

But I have love, and I have happiness.

In school tomorrow I'll find out if that's enough.

I'm strong now.

And I think — yes — that's enough.

About the Author

CAROLINE B. COONEY has written nearly seventy books for young people, including *Freeze Tag, Fatality,* and The Losing Christina trilogy: *Fog, Snow,* and *Fire*. Her books have sold more than ten million copies and have been printed in many languages. She lives in Connecticut with three pianos, two computers, and lots and lots of books.

3242

"Here's my offer," he said. "You want to be beautiful? I will give you Aryssa's beauty."

Have Aryssa's beauty! Imagine that. Imagine waking up in the morning, looking in your mirror, and seeing Aryssa there! Imagine how the boys would admire; how the girls would envy!

Aryssa's beauty.

"But what about Aryssa?"

"What about her?"

"What will she have?"

He smiled. The teeth were immense and sharp. "What she deserves," he said.

Also by Caroline B. Cooney